Vienna Spring:
Early Novellas and Stories

Studies in Austrian Literature, Culture and Thought
Translation Series

General Editors:

Jorun B. Johns
Richard H. Lawson

Stefan Zweig

Vienna Spring
Early Novellas and Stories

Translated and with an Afterword
by William Ruleman

ARIADNE PRESS
Riverside, California

Ariadne Press would like to express its appreciation to the
Bundesministerium für Unterricht, Kunst und Kultur for assistance in
publishing this book.

.KUNST

Translated from the German:
Ein Verbummelter, Die Liebe der Erika Ewald, Zwei Einsame,
Praterfrühling, Scharlach
© Williams Verlag, Zurich, 1976

Library of Congress Cataloging-in-Publication Data

Zweig, Stefan, 1881-1942.
 [Short stories. English. Selections]
 Vienna spring : early novellas and stories / Stefan Zweig ;
translated and with an afterword by William Ruleman.
 p. cm. -- (Studies in Austrian literature, culture, and thought.
 Translation series)
 Includes bibliographical references.
 ISBN 978-1-57241-173-9 (alk. paper)
 1. Zweig, Stefan, 1881-1942--Translations into English.
 2. Vienna (Austria)--Fiction. I. Ruleman, William. II. Title.
PT2653.W42A2 2010
833'.912--dc22
                            2010040101

Cover Design
Beth Steffel
Portrait by William Ruleman

Copyright 2010
by Ariadne Press
270 Goins Court
Riverside, CA 92507

All rights reserved.
No part of this publication may be reproduced or transmitted
in any form or by any means without formal permission.
Printed in the United States of America.
ISBN 978-1-57241-173-9

Contents

A Loser 3

Two Lonely Souls 9

The Love of Erika Ewald 13

Spring in the Prater 55

Scarlet Fever 67

Afterword 125

A LOSER

Passing the church tower clock, he saw it was high time to get to class. So he tucked his books snugly under his arm and quickened his pace. But soon he slackened his stride once more. The noon summer heat had made him sluggish. And really, it didn't seem that important to be on time for Greek. So he plodded on with a careless shrug on the cobblestones, which hurled up a smothering heat.

Once there, he saw he was ten or so minutes late. He briefly considered turning back. But thoughts of the lecture he'd get at supper that night so pained him he felt he should go on to class. He heaved the door open and went on in.

His sudden appearance caused some sensation. He could hear, behind him, haughty giggles; and up front, he saw only scornful grins. Then too, at the lectern, the master blinked – with a smug sort of smile – and muttered as if in disdain:

"It really would be a miracle, Liebmann, if you were to show up on time for once. You show in lateness a diligence – a staying power – that otherwise escapes you."

Mixed with a deeper, raucous rumbling, the giggling buzzed through the room. All looked up at Liebmann, who merely stood still and said not a word. But he found it hard to stay calm as he passed the gleeful faces en route to his seat. Inside him seethed the same profound pain, the same suppressed rage, that he always felt when he suffered this pitiless scene. He opened his book quite mechanically, and not at all caring what page he was on, he stared at the black letters blankly until they whirled and quivered before his eyes. Every word, every sound began to blur. The room became one huge senseless noise that hurt his ears. Indifference, like a leaden weight, began to drag him down.

A pair of sun squiggles played in front of his bench. They danced like happy, laughing kids, splashing their hues all over his desk. He eyed them as if inquisitive. And yet he did not really see them. He daydreamed, absent-minded . . .

Only yesterday evening, a vision of his life as he lived it now had flashed before his eyes. Plodding home with his books, he had met his peers – lieutenants, university students – who were once his friends yet who greeted him now with a strange contempt, a silent reserve, and only because he still sat with the babies and had to put up with the pompous rot the masters spewed out.

Rage and despair rose up in his throat. He wanted to laugh. It seemed a miracle, didn't it – that he didn't just throw himself down like a toddler or else spring up and spit at them all?

By and by he calmed himself. He'd begun to dissect his pain. He picked it apart with the chill cruelty that only the deepest pain can give. Was he so alone with his fate? Others – thousands – suffered it too; yes, his was an everyday tragedy. But no one had suffered it quite as much as *he* had, he felt. Ah, he was a loser, he knew. And so much of life still to go!

The thought of that first test he'd failed came back to haunt him again and again. The master had *let* him fail, and quite callously. This was the same man now seated ten steps before him and hardly noticing him at all. This was the same man who maybe never in his life had thought for one minute, for even one second, about what he – with one careless move – had done. This was the man who'd shot him down and so cut short the soaring flight of someone on his way up in the world. This was the man who'd taken a human life, and, with a careless shove, forced it onto a totally different track . . .

Liebmann still recalled – and quite well – the drastic change that had taken place when he'd lost a year for the very first time. His diligence (if not always effective, at least intense) had slackened slowly to apathy, gloom. And his love for art and poetry? All that had been hacked to pieces. He'd felt the brunt of that blow right about the time that his body, at least, was at its peak. Bit by bit, all his drive for his work had been snuffed out. More and more, he'd felt his creative fire go up in smoke – drowned by daydreams attractive to none but him, smothered by arid fantasies that fashioned for him a thousand shapes and goals that, in actual life, he could never hope to win: he no longer had the strength.

So he'd slowly begun to grow lazy and sink. Losing a year for the second time, he'd no longer felt it at all, though in passing he'd noticed he could not check his descent. Still on the school bench at twenty-one! That was the one disgrace he could not live down and that made him forget all the rest. He always found himself rooting round for the cause – returning, again and again, to one point: to that day when through chance, and *only* through chance, he had failed the exam. And bit by bit his steady brooding had blossomed into a much darker thought – a pale and baseless assumption, yes, but one that his morbid and violent musings had nonetheless branded to certainty – that no, it could *not* have been chance at all. A secret hatred must have compelled the master. The man had a hidden motive. Since then, this belief had taken deep root. Hate sounded the innermost depths of his soul.

The flooding force of this feeling caused him to shake whenever he looked at the man. Just sitting up there all smug with his pasty pastor's face – how *two*-faced and dull he was, dishing out nonsense with his fat voice – and all with a pompous solemnity that never admitted its own mistakes! And this man, they said, was *competent*. This man was supposed to command him – to decide his fate – and *had*, in fact. The thought strained all his nerves to a painful pitch as, unawares, he balled one fist and glared at the man, eyes glowing with hate.

The master turned and met those eyes. Though he seemed to notice nothing, the rims of his mouth began to crinkle – with that hard and sullen look. Then he said, with utter indifference:

"Liebmann, you'd do better if you would only look at your book and pay attention, instead of just gaping into thin air."

Liebmann flinched. To be lectured to like this! The thought scorched like a glowing match. Defiance leapt up in him. He wouldn't be silenced this time!

"I *have* paid attention, sir!"

"All the better for you, Liebmann. Repeat what I was saying, then."

These words were calmly uttered, and likely, with no ill intent. But Liebmann felt a mean spite in them. He knew not a word of what had been said, and he frantically bit his lips. But a dark foreboding awoke in him. A crisis could issue forth from this trifle. Fate hoped that the cruel daily game be repeated: it could draw, from the meanest detail, unforeseen results. He knew it would have to come to something: he felt within all the courage, despair – all the stifled hate of countless hours – now merging into one broad gushing stream determined to force its way.

And yet he controlled it. Lips pale and quivering, he kept still.

The master waited some seconds. Then he said, with no trace of tension:

"You know nothing, then, and have lied just now."

That was what clinched it. Now there was no more turning back. His was a lost cause, he knew. But he knew, as well, that all the emotion dammed up inside him would have to be voiced – if not today, then tomorrow. And into the bargain, his classmates' giggling was only mounting, goading him on. Just not to belong to this anymore! Let come what would ... His voice rang clear and determined.

"I *did* not lie. I *could* repeat it."

"You don't want to, then?"

"No, I don't. It was all just nonsense and garbage."

The words struck the classroom like lightning. The smiles that had listened with smug expectation now fell. All felt here, in this thunder-charged air, a crisis of far-reaching import.

Liebmann himself was the calmest. He'd reached a firm conclusion because he had willed it. It had happened now.

The master by now had won back the composure he'd lost in the wake of the unforeseen insult. Stepping quickly up to Liebmann, he said, voice gasping and trembling with rage:

"You cheeky ..."

"Cheeky yourself!"

Liebmann's words cut short the master's own. Chaos and stress ensued, as if from a scuffle. None could tell who raised a hand first, but the rage in both was so frenzied and urgent that only brute and instinctive force could express it. The whole scene lasted only a second: with the uttermost strength of his hate, Liebmann struck the other with such a blow that he staggered back. The room filled with noise; the boys sprang up in blind excitement. Yet before they could intervene, Liebmann had torn his hat from the hook and stormed out, the door slamming shut behind him. He was out, only out without goal or plan . . .

He roamed for an hour or so before he could clear his head and resolve on a course to take. He'd seen it all: a thousand garish sights had met his eyes – scenes of his youth, his future, his parents – yet his act had so transfigured them that each was only a signpost guiding him toward his last dark path. As if by instinct, he'd quickened his pace and started to run. Little hopes and vague surmises dashed up before him with lightning-like speed. Yet he did not retain them – just ran and ran. His ears rang from the roar of cars, the noise of the street, the hum of people who glided past, unheeding and unaware of him, as well as from his own panting. He ran faster and faster, as if to deafen all thought, and his whole brain hummed but a single phrase: "Just quickly, quickly . . ." All around him rang to the rhythm of these words, joining to form a chaotic roar that numbed and stupefied him.

And so he came to the bridge. There he stood for a moment, though not from fear, but only because his trembling arm lacked the strength to hurl him over the rail. Images of his ruined life rose before his eyes once more; with a sudden jolt, his whole body shuddered. With one swing he was over the rail and dashing, whistling down like lightning into the rushing gray flood . . .

TWO LONELY SOULS

The mass of factory workers surged through the gate like a broad and rushing stream. On the street, the crowd dammed up for a moment as farewells and brief handshakes were exchanged. Then the separate clusters wandered on toward their separate abodes, crumbling into smaller components here and there on the way. Still, on the big country road to town, all drew tighter in a vivid muddle of loud, glad voices that faded with uniform dullness. The girls' bright laughter alone rang out in the evening stillness like a pewter bell.

Lagging behind the clustered group, one worker trudged on alone. He was not yet old and by no means puny, but he couldn't keep up their pace: his lame foot wouldn't allow it. The happy voices still rang from afar; he listened with no sense of pain. His affliction had long inured him to loneliness, and loneliness made him reticent: a philosopher who looked on life with all the indifference of one who does without.

He slowly limped on. From the dark, distant fields came a full, warm air of early ripeness the evening mist could not dispel. The distant laughter died away. Now a lone cricket chirped. Otherwise, all was still, with that deep, sad silence wherein hidden thoughts begin to speak.

Then his ears pricked. He seemed to hear someone crying. He listened in the stillness. All was quiet, as if in dreamless sleep. But a moment later he heard it again – a moan – much sharper now, and full of pain. And in the vague dusk he saw a shape that sat crying there beside the road on a heap of stacked railway tracks. Drawing nearer, he recognized her, the girl who was sobbing incessantly.

She worked at the same factory he did. He knew her there as the one they called "ugly Jula," for her looks made her stand out so much that she'd suffered this name ever since she was little. Her face was coarse and misshapen, with skin so dirty yellow in hue as to make her seem repulsive. With it came a marked disharmony in her build: an emaciated upper torso, weak as a child's, which rose from broad and rather curved hips. The only beautiful thing about her was her calm and brilliant eyes, which countered every look of loathsome scorn with a mild humility.

He himself had already borne too much secret sorrow to be able to pass her by without pity. And so, stepping closer, he laid his hand soothingly on her shoulder.

"Let me be!"

She did not know to whom she had spoken and had merely cried out wildly in her pain.

Now, recognizing the stranger, she grew calmer. She knew him because he was one of the few in the factory who'd never mocked her. But she only murmured more defensively:

"Let me be, I say! Let me be! I'll sort it out by myself!"

He said nothing but sat down beside her. Her sobs only grew more severe and frantic. Yet he spoke consolingly to her:

"Don't be like that, Jula! Crying won't make it better!"

She was silent. He asked carefully:

"So . . . What have they done to you now?"

The question called her back to herself. Blood suddenly shot up to her cheeks, and her words were rushed as she quickly related:

"After work, as we're going home, they're all talking of how tomorrow's Sunday. They all want to go to the country – out into the villages there. One of them makes the suggestion, and right away, they're all for it. And as the votes are being counted, I'm so stupid I hold my hand up too. Of course they laugh and start up their nasty jeering again, and they carry on so bad – as never before – that before you know it I'm going wild. And I don't know what happened with me – I lost my patience and suddenly told them what vile things they were. And then – they hit me."

She lapsed back into her sudden sobbing. He was deeply moved and felt the need to say a few words; so, to comfort her, he began to tell the story of one of his own misfortunes.

"Look, Jula, you mustn't have such wicked thoughts. So what if tomorrow you're going out into the fields all alone? There are some who on Sunday can't keep up. Some who can't even once go out alone, because their feet can hardly carry them from the factory to town. Some who don't have such an easy life either, who always have to limp and so are always alone because it's too boring for any of the rest to go with them. You have no right to such wicked thoughts, Jula! And all toward a few dumb characters like them!"

She quickly resisted him, not wishing to diminish or abandon the pain and the martyrdom that all who suffer feel.

"They're not the ones who make me sick. It's everything – my whole life. At times, when I see myself this way, it all comes over me like disgust. Why am I so ugly? I can't do anything about it. Yet I've suffered it my whole life. Ever since I was little, I've had to feel that they were laughing at me. And because of that, I've never wanted to play with others because I've been afraid of them and envied them."

He listened, quivering, while she revealed all this pain – pain that he understood so well. For that stored-up grief of a thousand dreadful hours he'd long thought dead now woke again from its sleep. (He'd long since forgotten he needed comforting here.) And so, spontaneously, he also told of his own fate, for now he had found someone who could understand. Gently, he began:

"Once there was one who also wished to play with the others, but he could not. One who, whenever they romped and leaped, always limped behind with difficulty. One who always showed up everywhere too late. One who was always so helpless and clumsy, which caused the others to laugh at him. One who maybe has it worse off than you with your healthy legs that can go anywhere in the whole wide world."

This only increased her agitation. She felt all the pain of her life break forth.

"*No one* could have it worse than I do! No one's ever said a good word to me! I never even knew my mother! While every other girl passes by with her boy, here *I* am all alone! And I feel it will always be like that and will have to be, even when I feel as the others do! God! If I just knew why it's *so*!"

What they had never said to anyone, what they had hardly admitted even to themselves, these two – who were still nearly strangers – now revealed. Every cry of their souls found an echo now, for they shared a kindred sorrow. He told her how he had never had a girl – and why? Because he never dared go up to one with his slowly dragging foot! Because not a one of them wanted to walk so carefully with him! He explained how he had to fend for himself – how filthy wenches just *tossed* his weekly wages at him, how every day he just grew sadder and more tired of life . . .

The sound of steps disrupted their sad confessions. A couple walked up, their shadows too weak and uncertain to recognize. As they moved on past, he rose and said, with a simple plea:

"Come on."

She went. By now it had grown quite dark. No longer now could he see her face. And, in her gentle sense of forlornness and pain, she did not sense at first that her gait had passed his own. But then she noticed and slowed her pace and walked along at his side. A blind understanding had settled over this lonely pair like a blessing. Their words grew gentler, more intimate; and they had to bend close together so each could hear what the other said.

All at once she noted, with a vague joy, how his hand reached round her swollen hips in a soft and groping caress . . .

THE LOVE OF ERIKA EWALD

To Camill Hoffmann

In profound friendship

. . . But that is the story of all young girls, these ones who suffer gently, in silence. They never say that they suffer. Women are made for suffering. It is, to be certain, so much a part of their destiny, they experience it so early and are so little surprised by it, that again and again, they say, there is no illness here, when in fact it set in a long time ago . . .

— Barbey d'Aurévilly

Erika Ewald went in slowly, with the light and careful step of one arriving late. Her father and sister were already at supper; at the sound of the door, they looked up to give a passing nod at the one coming in; then the clink of plates, and the clatter of knives, resounded once more through the ill-lit room. Talk was rare; only now and then did a word fall, to flutter feebly — like a leaf tossed into the air — then sink, fatigued, to the floor. They all had little to say to one another. Her sister was plain, even downright ugly; and years of being scorned or ignored had dealt her that brooding and old-maidish air of defeat that watches each day fade with a smile. A long and bland career in the business world had made their father a stranger; and especially since the death of his wife, he'd enclosed himself in that same hard, stubborn, disgruntled silence with which the elderly hide their bodies' complaints.

Erika, too, was chiefly silent on these tedious evenings. She felt she could not let herself contend with the gray mood that lay like thick and threatening storm clouds over the house. And then, she was much too tired for it. The torture of her day's work, which hour by hour compelled her to suffer the groping, dissonant chords of her students, triggered, as always, a dull need for calm — a wordless exuding of every feeling the day's ceaseless might had beat down. She loved to entrust herself to those waking dreams, for an almost over-excited shyness allowed her to show to others no more than a hint of her spirit's affairs, even if that same spirit quivered beneath the pressure of her unspoken words, much as the boughs of an over-ripe fruit tree shudder beneath the weight of its treasures. And only a fine and light and nearly imperceptible tension about the pale, thin lips betrayed the struggle that went on inside her, as well as an unrestrained yearning that would not let itself be uttered in words, so that, at times, a wild trembling played round the firmly-shut lips, as if from sudden, held-back sobs.

Soon supper was over. Her father got up, said a curt goodnight, went into his room and lit his pipe. And as always, her sister grabbed her sewing things and, crouching far forward in her short-sightedness, commenced to stitch by the lamplight like a machine . . . It was like that every night in this house, where the most trivial of actions fossilized into rigid routines.

Erika went to her room and slowly began to undress. It was getting late. On other evenings she tended to read well into the night, or else she leaned at the window wistfully and looked out onto the rooftops bathed in the bright silver flood of the moon. Her thoughts at those times were never of striving or clear aims or goals. Instead, they were merely vague feelings of love for the shimmering, flashing, yet gently exuding streams of moonlight that countless windows mirrored even as they hid life's secrets behind their panes. But tonight she felt a mild fatigue, a blissful heaviness that made her long to snuggle under warm and gentle blankets. Like a softly chilling and numbing poison, there coursed through her limbs a sleepiness that was nothing less than a longing for sweet and heavenly dreams. She roused herself, threw the rest of her clothes off almost in haste, and snuffed out her candle. A moment yet – and then she stretched herself out in bed.

Like a nimble play of shadows, the joyful memories of the day danced past yet again. Today she had been with *him* . . . Again they'd rehearsed for her concert together, with him as accompanist. Then he'd played Chopin – the "Ballad Without Words" – for her. And the kind, gentle words he'd spoken to her, the many lovely words!

The images rushed past faster and faster, calling her back to herself before they strayed back into the past again, to the day when she had first met him. Then they stormed out over the straits of her life, the limits of time, to wax ever wilder, more garish. She heard her sister go to bed next door. And an odd and crazy thought came to her: had he even asked her to come visit him? A happy and spirited smile endeavored to creep its way wearily over her lips, but she was already much too drunk with sleep. Mere moments later, a sure and steady slumber bore her away to blissful dreams.

On waking, she found a postcard on her bed. Only a few words had been scribbled upon it, dashed down with a firm, energetic hand. They were words such as those one might throw away on a stranger. But Erika felt them a lucky gift, for he'd written them to *her*. She was led to infer – from these trivial, inconspicuous words – a premonition of true fulfillment. And as such, this love would be more than a soft radiance: it would be like a halo illuminating everything. Indeed, so deeply would she absorb it – this feeling that transfigured all around her – that it would swell like a glimmer that seemed to expand from every soulless and empty aspect of her life. Since early youth she had known, from the dark elements in her anxious nature – from her ever-guarded solitude – not to view mere objects as cold and lifeless but as silent friends in whom to confide the affections and secrets she held within. Books and pictures, pieces of music and landscapes – all of these spoke to Erika, in whom the poetic capacity of a child had remained, enabling her to see, in painted dolls and other inanimate things, a motley reality, and be moved. And such were her lonely banquets and blessings before this love had come to her.

So too did the little black pen strokes upon the card become, for her, an event. She read the words as he tended to speak to her – with the soft and musical tone of his voice. She sought to imbed in their characters the sweetly secret charm that only tender speech can give. And, for the very reason that their letters were couched in cool and almost respectable form, she heard in the little phrases the hidden, resounding undertone of a love spelled out so slowly and dreamily that she had nearly forgotten their contents, which in themselves were not that important. "Would she care to inform him whether the outing they'd planned for Sunday would still take place?" they said. Then he'd dashed down a word or two about their joint appearance in a long-discussed concert, and after that, a hasty signature's friendly close. But she read the lines again and again, believing that she could hear in them a strong and urgent emotion that really only echoed her own.

It had not been long since this love had first come to Erika Ewald and shone its luster upon her vague and indifferent existence. And its history was quiet and commonplace.

They had met at a reception – one held by a society for which she merely gave piano lessons, although her discreet and delicate way had so endeared her to all that she was seen as more than a friend. And he'd been invited to an event as the pièce de résistance so to speak, for his repute as a virtuoso violinist was highly exceptional, in spite of his youth.

The circumstances proved quite willing to support an understanding. He was asked to play, and it seemed only natural that she should accompany him. And that was when he first took notice of her, for she played with such a grasp of his intentions that he instantly sensed her nature's intensity and refinement. And right in the midst of the stormy applause that followed the performance, he proposed to her that they have a chat. She nodded faintly – quite imperceptibly.

But it did not come to that. They were not set free so quickly: he could only eye her supple, overly slender figure from time to time with stolen glances to seize a shy and astonished greeting from her dark eyes. Their words were submerged in petty niceties that overwhelmed them. Then new people came, and a hundred and one distractions of another sort, so that they almost forgot their arrangement to meet. But when everything was over, and she was about to leave, he was suddenly standing beside her and asking, with his gentle, guarded voice, whether she would allow him to escort her home. For a moment, she was helpless. Then she declined his offer so clumsily that he was able at last, and quite easily, to receive her consent.

She lived rather far out in the suburbs, and it was a long way there in the clear and moonlit night. For a long time, a silence lay between them. This was not awkwardness on their part, but the uncertain dread that refined and highly-developed natures have of beginning a conversation with banalities. At last he began to speak – of the piece they had played together, then of art in general. But that was just the beginning – only a way to her soul, for he knew that she guarded, concealed the whole rich hoard of her feeling in musical beauty, regally squandered her life's every treasure on art – a fact betrayed to those like him, who understood. And in her views on creating and interpreting, she actually disclosed to him many of her secret spiritual adventures – several of which she had never confided to anyone, and some of which, up till now, she herself had not even been conscious. Later, when he'd grown closer to her, and become her confidant and friend, even she would not be able to grasp how she'd overcome her constant, almost anxious restraint of that time. For on that evening an artist, a creator, still seemed to her like some Colossus who never enters life but resides far off – aloof, inaccessible – one from whom nothing can be concealed. Up till now only simple people had entered her sphere – people who could be analyzed simply and summed up like grade school exercises: biased, conformist finger-pointers who were strangers to her, whom she almost feared. Then too, it was such a bright, still night . . . And when one walks with another on such a night, unheard by others and undisturbed, when the houses' dim shadows sink down on one's words – and when voices scatter, echoless, on the silence – then one is as richly confident as if one were talking to oneself. Then thoughts awake from the depths that in the motley unrest of the day are submerged, unheard – thoughts to which the night's stillness gives gentle wings. And thoughts grow into words – almost against one's will.

The long walk in the winter night had brought her close to another. When they extended their hands in farewell, her pale, cool fingers lay helpless in his firm hand's grip for a long while, as if forgotten. And they departed like old friends.

They ran into each other quite often that winter – first by convenient coincidence, but soon by prior arrangement. This girl, with all her strange eccentricities, intrigued and excited him. He admired the noble reserve of her soul, which she revealed to him alone – hurling it hesitantly at his feet, like a frightened child. He loved her myriad subtleties. He loved the simple force of her feeling that led her, so weak of will, toward everything lovely and yet could hide itself from strangers' eyes so as not to disturb the pure depths of her pleasure. But these tender and intimate feelings, which he could have shared with anyone (and just as richly and thrillingly) were alien to him. For, as an artist, he had been spoiled. From his youth on up, while still half a child, he had been too pampered by women, too much led astray, to be satisfied by a spiritual love. There was far too little of the feminine or the boyish in him, and the whole naïve and sweet contentment of teenage love had never crept into his precocious life. Blasé and high-spirited at the same time, he loved with that brusque desire that craves the ultimate in sensual fulfillment in order to spend itself completely. And he knew himself, and he held in contempt every weakness that overwhelmed him. He looked with disgust on his hasty gratifications, though he could not defend himself against them. For sensual passion coursed through his life like his art. The mastery of his playing was rooted in this hard and vital manliness. He forced every last and fading nuance – like the faint breaths of a slumbering sadness – to flee the frenzied yet gypsy-sweet stirrings of his bow. The enthralling force of his playing subdued and concealed something soft and timid in him.

And her love for him was just so submissive and timid. She loved in his person all the forms of her dreams, which, in her long years of solitude, had attained a certain reality. She honored the artist embodied in his being, for she held the girlish belief that an artist must demonstrate, in his way of life, the dignity of a priest. At times she stared at him with an odd and absurdly searching gaze, as if at an alien image in which one wishes to find familiar features. Her admissions to him were as to a confessor. She did not think of life, for she had never known it – only experienced it like a dream that has no basis in reality. Because of that, she lacked every care and fear for the future. Instead, she believed in a mild and blissful continuation of her love, this irrationally adoring love she had formed, with so much confidence, through her inner purity and aesthetic sense of beauty.

At times she surprised herself that she felt no need to speak when alone with him. He either played or was silent while she sat and dreamed and just felt those dreams wax ever lighter, ever brighter, while he talked or she gazed at him. All else had faded; no stray noise from the day pressed in on them here – only silence, stillness, and silver holiday bells deep in the heart. And a yearning need for affection, an expectation of loving and gentle words (which she actually feared) now quivered within her. She sensed how, as she fell utterly under his spell, he could master her with his artistry, give pain and joy both with his tempting sounds. She felt helpless before his playing, and unspeakably poor, for she could give nothing, could only receive – and beg from him – with open, trembling hands.

It had now become a habit – quite irreversible – for her to visit him more and more during the week. At first this was just to rehearse a joint concert. But soon they could not do without these few hours. She did not at all foresee the danger that lay in this growing intimacy. Instead, she let the last restraint of her soul fall before him and reveal to him, as her only friend, her most hidden secrets. In the midst of her heated and almost visionary narratives, she often hardly noticed that he, in mounting agitation, embraced her hands and at times even lowered his burning lips to her fingers while he lay at her feet and listened. Nor did she note when he at times, with the most urgent and demanding strains of his violin, spoke only to her, for she was ever seeking herself, and her dreams, in his music. This time was one of understanding and release of the many things that up till then she had never dared to say aloud, but so far it was nothing more. She knew only that such a quiet hour brought untold splendor into her desolate, work-crammed day, as well as a shimmering radiance to her nights. And she wished for no more than a blissful silence, a rich peacefulness, to which she could flee as to an altar.

But she took good care not to show her happiness openly. Before her family and others, her lips often hid a smile of pure bliss with such severe force as to leave her on the verge of sobs. For she wished to shield her adventure from alien stares, as if she were guarding something precious – a work of art with hundreds of fragile facets – from clumsy fingers that would shatter it with a frightened shriek. And she coddled her life and her bliss in cool, clichéd words just so they could pass through many hands without being cheapened and smashed into so many worthless shards.

On Saturday evening before their outing, she went to see him again. As she tapped at his door, she felt once again that odd apprehension she always felt when she went to him, a feeling that mounted more and more until he appeared. But she did not have long to wait. He soon arrived and led her into his study, removed her spring coat with careful gallantry, and respectfully brushed her lovely and finely-veined hand with his lips. And then they sat down together on a small dark velvet sofa beside his writing desk.

The room was already getting dark. Outside, gray clouds hastily trailed one another in the evening wind, their shadows fitfully dimming the weak twilight. He asked whether he should turn on a light. She said no. The soft, weak glow that allows no clarity of sight – only sensing – was as pleasant to her as his melancholy. One could still discern clearly the room's furnishings: the splendid writing desk with its bronze statue, and, to its right, an ornately-carved violin stand, silhouetted sharply against the sliver of gray sky peering in, with utter indifference, through the windowpanes. Somewhere a clock ticked with hard, measured beats, like the firm steps of pitiless time. Otherwise, all was still. Only a few bluish wisps from his forgotten cigarette arose, flowing elegantly in the darkness. And a tepid spring wind wafted in to them.

They talked. First it was all mere jokes and smiles. However, with the impending darkness, their words grew more and more solemn. He spoke of a new composition, a song of love based on a stanza or two from a simple folk song he had heard in a village once. Two girls had been coming in from work, their voices resounding from such a distance he'd not been able to grasp their words – only heard the soft and gravely-inspiring longing revealed in the melody. And yesterday, late in the evening, that melody had wakened in him once more, becoming a song for him.

She said nothing – only gazed at him. And he understood her plea. In silence he stepped to the window and took his violin. His song commenced quite gently.

Behind him the scene slowly brightened again. The evening clouds caught fire and glowed in crimson splendor. The room began to shine again from the radiant gleam that by and by grew murkier, more replete.

He played the sad song with marvelous force, losing himself in its sounds. And then he abandoned his own composition, retaining only the eerie and endlessly longing folk tune that, in his variations, stammered, wept, and rejoiced by turns. He no longer thought about anything; his musings were distant, confused; now only the stream of his spirit's feeling formed the sounds, surrendering itself to them. The dark, narrow room overflowed with beauty. The fiery red clouds had now become gloomy black shadows, yet he played on.

For a long time now, he'd forgotten that he was playing this song as an homage only to her. His passion for every embodiment of beauty – his love for every woman in the world – awoke in the strings, which shuddered in blissful ardor. Again and again, he found a fresh intensity and a wilder force, but never the transfiguring fulfillment; in its furious upward spiraling, it ever remained only yearning: moaning and yet exultant longing. And he played on and on, as if toward a certain chord, a conclusive solution he could not find.

All at once he broke off abruptly . . . Ecstatic – as if bewitched by the sounds – Erika had risen from the sofa, but now she collapsed back onto it with muffled and yet hysterical sobs. Her weak and easily excitable nerves were ever subject to music's allure; wistful tunes could make her cry. And this song – with all its urgency, all its lashing flames of expectation – had roused within her every emotion, stunned her nerves with one breathtaking jolt. She felt the frightful force of her submerged longing plunge up from within like agony – sensed she would have to scream from the thrust of all this constricted pain; but she could not. Her mounting bodily agitation could only dissolve in a spasm of sobs.

He knelt beside her and sought to calm her. Quite gently, he kissed her hand. But she kept on shaking, and at times a twitch ran over her fingers like an electric shock. He addressed her with friendly words. She did not hear. Then he grew more fervent and, with heated words now, began to kiss her fingers, her hand, and her quivering mouth, which shuddered instinctively under his lips. His kisses grew more urgent as, gasping tender words of love, he caressed her with ever stormier, more demanding embraces.

All at once she emerged from her half-dreaming state and pushed him back almost violently. He got up, shocked and uncertain. For a moment yet, she kept silent, as if recalling all around her. Then, with a restless look and a broken voice, she stammered her hope that he might forgive her, that she often had nervous attacks like this, that the music must have provoked her.

For a moment, a painful silence loomed in the air. He dared not reply, afraid that he might have played a despicable role.

She then added that she would have to go: they'd have long been expecting her home by now. In the same breath, she took her coat. Her voice seemed cool – almost icy – to him.

He longed to say something, but it all seemed so ridiculous to him after the words he'd just spoken in all his besotted passion. In silent respect, he escorted her to the door. Not till he kissed her hand in farewell did he timidly ask her:

"And tomorrow?"

"As we've planned. Am I thinking right?"

"That goes without saying."

He was joyfully calmed that she went away with no word about his behavior. He also admired her refined restraint, which forgave that behavior by taking no note of it. Each said a brief farewell. Then he quietly shut and locked the door.

Sunday morning had been a bit cloudy and glum. Early on, heavy fog had enmeshed the city within its thick web, and, through delicate chinks, permitted a soft spray of rain to shiver down onto the street. But soon it began to sparkle inside that dark web, as if a crown of gold, which shimmered and brightened more and more, had been captured therein. And at last the cloudy membrane tore beneath the burden of light, and a fresh spring sun came shining down, its youthful face mirrored a thousand times in the glittering puddles, the gently-glowing church tower cupolas, the dazzling windows and shiny wet roofs, and the cheerful looks of those now peering onto it all.

By noon the streets teemed with Sunday's bright hustle and bustle. The rattling carriages clattered a glad melody, the tram signal shrilled in bright turmoil, and the sparrows that shrieked from the telegraph wires believed they could outdo both. Daring now, for the first time that year, to show themselves out of doors again, a flood of people surged toward the suburbs, oozing onto the main avenues like a dark sea shimmering with gaudy spring clothes and hues. And over them all lay the sun – a bright, flooding spring sun with flashing gleam.

Erika was thrilled to be out like this. She gaily strolled with him arm in arm and even found herself wishing that she could dance and frolic about like a child. Indeed, she *looked* quite childlike and girlish today in her plain, simple clothing and pinned-up hair, which usually loomed above her brow as brooding and deep as a rain-turgid cloud. And so gushing yet genuine was her glee, he soon shook off his own solemn mood.

They'd soon abandoned their first, spontaneous thoughts of entering the Prater, for they shied away from the shrill Sunday hubbub that breaks that grand old park's solemn silence. *Their* Prater – that meant broad and well-tended lanes; ancient, majestic chestnut trees; broad, roaming meadows that end in dark woods; and bright fields that bask in the sun-sated gleam and know nothing at all of the million-hearted city that breathes and groans right next door. But on Sundays, this magic was lost – concealed by the flooding hordes.

He proposed that they head toward Döbling, then far beyond that nice little place with its friendly white houses that coquettishly flaunt their bright, trim gardens in the midst of dark surroundings. He knew of one or two silent and intimate paths that gently led, through slender lanes of clipped acacias in bloom, into some spacious fields.

So that was the route they took today. Arriving in that silent place, with its almost rustic Sunday peace, which shadowed them throughout their walk like a mild and inexplicable fragrance, they eyed each other at times and felt how rich their silence was, how it bore and enhanced the whole blissful sense of fully-flowing spring.

The fields were still low and green. But the warm and giving earth, with its blessedly-heavy scent, rose up to them like a promise. Far off stood the Kahlenberg and the Leopoldsberg, with their little old churches before whose walls the slopes plunge into the Danube. In between lay much fertile land, most still brown and untilled and full of sown seed. But even in the midst of this, square patches of waxing golden fruit – like the worn, torn rags on the tanned and powerful torso of a hard-working laborer – rose sharply and unexpectedly from the dark abundance of the earth. And overhead, a cheery spring sky spanned like a blue arch in which spry and twittering swallows sailed.

As they came through the lane of acacias, he spoke of how this had been Beethoven's favorite path, the place where, while walking, the master had first felt the inspiration for so many of his most profound creations. The name put both in a sober mood. They thought of music, which had, in so many gracious hours, enriched and deepened their lives. All seemed grander and much more important now as they walked along, thinking of him: they felt the majesty of the landscape, whose joy and clarity till now they had only *seen*; they breathed in the heavy and sated scents of the earth, which glowed with sun and swelled with fruit and hinted at spring's deepest mysteries.

Their path ran on through the fields. In passing along, Erika knelt and let the green grain rustle its way through her fingers. When a blade nicked her hand, she did not feel a thing. The silence between them lent her curious thoughts, deep reflections she lost herself in, as if in a dream. Mild and mysterious feelings of love were awakened in her. Yet she did not think of the one who walked by her side, but of all that was and that lived – of the grain that softly waved in the wind, of the people to whom it gave joy and work, of the swallows that chased one another through the air, and of the city, which gazed over at them, enclosed in a veil of gray haze far below. Like a child who, for the very first time, leaps forth, rejoicing, into the gently-streaming light of the sun, she felt inside her, once again, the all-embracing power of spring.

They walked a long time in the meadows and fields. Meanwhile the afternoon inclined toward its end. It was not yet evening, though by and by, the sharp light drifted over into a softly-fading lassitude that foretold its presence close at hand, and a tone of pale rose trembled on the air. Erika had grown a little tired, and, from a wish to rest but also from curiosity, they entered a little inn along the way from which glad voices, in lively confusion, rang out toward them. They sat down in the garden. At neighboring tables sat suburban families with friendly features and loud, free voices – good folk of a "better sort" who, in the Viennese way, celebrated their Sundays with a jaunt. In the shade behind them lurked some musicians, three or four men who on weekdays traipsed round begging and only on Sundays enjoyed a roof over their heads. But they played the trite old folk tunes quite well, and when they began an especially dashing favorite, soon every voice joined in and sang along in full force. Even the ladies chimed in; none was shy. Here all was cozy comfort, complacent contentment.

Erika smiled at him across the table, but quite stealthily, so that no one would feel insulted. These plain, uncomplicated people, with their simple feelings and urges that they could not conceal, pleased both of them. And this snug rustic mood, unspoiled by outside influences, pleased them as well.

The landlord, a broad, good-natured fellow, stepped up to them with a jovial smile. He'd noticed, among his guests, someone distinguished – a young man he wished to serve himself. Might he have the pleasure of bringing some wine? When the answer was yes, he also inquired whether this young lady – the young man's bride – wished for something, as well.

Erika blushed. At first, she did not know how to reply. Then she merely nodded, bewildered. Her "bridegroom" sat there across from her, and though she did not look at him, she could still feel his smiling gaze, which feasted on her confusion. She reddened with shame. How clumsy she was acting! And all because of a natural mistake! Still, she could not shake off her painful emotions. All at once, her good mood was ruined. Only now did she feel how mechanical and choppy these people sounded, humming away at their maudlin songs; only now could she hear the ugly roar of the beery basses, howling along in mad delight. Now she wanted only to leave.

Then the fiddler began a few eerie rhythms. With soft, sweet strokes, he played an old waltz by Johann Strauss. The others gently joined in on the soft, dear tune. Once again, Erika was spellbound by the compelling force that music exerted upon her soul, for all at once she felt at ease, as if she were gently rocking or floating. And the melody's sweetness led her to hum, to sing along (though very gently) the curious lyrics without really knowing she was doing so. She just felt all was good and happy again. Indeed, she felt spring in bloom again, as well as her own dancing heart.

With the waltz's ending, he stood up to leave. She gladly followed, understanding his wish not to let the melody's thrilling power, as well as their sunny intimacy, be destroyed by some dreary popular tune. So they walked the lovely way back to the city again.

The sun had already sunk. And yet, from beyond the mountains' rims, through the trees laced round with glowing gold, strange and delicate rivulets of rose-hued light were seeping down into the valley. The sight was marvelous. A reddish gleam loomed in the sky – like a distant conflagration. Far below it, a richly-hued and radiant haze arched over the city like a crimson globe. Now, with evening, all sounds blended in milder harmony: the distant singing of Sunday excursionists, accompanied by a harmonica; the ever-mounting stitch of crickets; and the uncertain whistle and murmur that whispered in every branch, lived in every leaf, and even seemed to hum on the air.

All at once, quite abruptly, he spilled some words into their solemn and almost devout silence.

"You know, Erika, it was really funny the way the landlord called you my bride."

Then he laughed – in a strained, forced way.

Erika woke from her daydream. What did he mean by that? He seemed to want to start something, to force a conversation. She felt a fear within her – a dumb and senseless angst – and gave no reply.

"No, really, wasn't that funny? And the way you blushed?"

She glanced at him – to observe his expression. Was he trying to make fun of her? No! He was really quite earnest and wasn't looking at her at all. But he did want an answer. And not till now did she feel how strained, how tentative his words had been when he'd said that. It frightened her; she did not know why. But she had to say something; he was waiting.

"To me it was far less funny than painful. I can't even understand the joke."

She spoke these words with a hard finality, as if she were irritated. Then a silence fell between them again. But no longer was it the blissful silence of mutual pleasure, the intimate sense of expectation, the apprehension of burgeoning feeling, they both had experienced earlier. It was, instead, a dark and brooding kind of silence, a silence suppressing something threatening and urgent. And all of a sudden she feared her love – feared it would grow as agonizing and all-consuming as every joy she had ever felt – the joys she drew from the mild, wistful books that were dearest to her; the very joys that made her weep; the joys that resembled the burning surges, the floods of sound, in *Tristan und Isolde*; the joys that meant the highest bliss yet pierced her through with pain. The silence oppressed her more and more. It bloomed like a dark and brooding fog that pressed down painfully on her eyes. Yet by and by she was freed of her terror. And she wished to question him clearly and frankly – and in doing so make an end to all this.

"You seem to want to keep me in the dark about something. What is it?"

He remained silent a moment. Then he eyed her with dark, immobile orbs. After turning aside to reflect, he eyed her once more, and now with more depth and certainty. His voice now seemed oddly full and melodic.

"I haven't known it long – only for a short time now. I . . . I long for you."

Erika shuddered. She'd turned her eyes to the ground, but still she felt him staring at her, with a look deeply probing, penetrating. She thought of their last time together – of how he had kissed her. She'd said nothing to him then, but her heart had been wakened abruptly. In anger? In shame? She didn't know. And the dread she usually felt when he played such glowing and passionate songs – that blissful terror with endless depths and blessings – seized her again. What would come now? Oh God, God! . . . She sensed that he'd go on talking, and she longed for and feared it too. She didn't want to hear it. She wanted to see the fields, the evening, the beautiful evening . . . Just to hear nothing, nothing. Just to gaze at the city with its dark mist – the city, the fields. And the clouds there, overhead . . . The clouds, how they sailed so fast through the sky! Quite a few were still up there, weren't there? One . . . two . . . three . . . four . . . five . . . Yes, five clouds . . . No! Just four! Yes, four . . .

But here he was talking again!

"I've feared my passion a long time now, Erika! I've always sensed it would overwhelm me someday. I just didn't want to believe it. Now it's here. I've known since yesterday – since the last time you were with me."

He was silent a moment. He held his breath deep down in his chest.

"And – that makes me sad – infinitely sad. I know I can't marry you. I know it would cost me my art. No stranger can understand that. But *you* will understand it – my lovely, lovely Erika. For only an artist can understand that. And you have the infinitely rich soul of an artist. And you're smart, along with it all. Well . . . We can't go on like this . . . It's all got to come to an end . . ."

He paused. She felt that he wasn't quite finished. She'd have liked to sink down before him – to beg him not to go on. She wished to hear nothing, to understand nothing. No, she didn't want . . . And, filled with fear, she began to count the clouds again . . .

But they were already far away . . . No, one cloud was still there . . . one, the last, suffused with rose, like a proud swan sailing down a dark stream . . . Why did that image occur to her? She didn't know . . . Her thoughts grew more and more confused. She just knew that she wanted to think only of that cloud . . . which was drifting away, over the mountain now . . . She felt that her whole heart clung to it, that she'd love to stop it with outstretched hands. But there it went . . . It sailed faster, faster . . . And now it had vanished . . . And she heard once again – irreversible, clear – his words, while her heart, in blind fear, shuddered.

"I don't know if you know me like that. I don't believe – I don't think – that you see me as more than I am. I'm not a great man, you know. I'm not one of those who . . . who stand above life in their self-sufficiency. I wanted to be like that, but I'm not. I cling to life. I'm really just one who desires what he loves. I'm like that – the way that every man is. I don't just worship a woman I love. I . . . crave her too . . . And . . . well, I won't cheat on you with strangers. Please don't despise me. You're too dear to me for that . . ."

Erika had turned pale. *Now* she saw what he meant . . . Why hadn't she thought of it earlier? All at once, she grew calm again. All had come, as it had to come.

She wanted to speak with words of rejection, but she could not. His lovely use of *du* – that sweet and intimate form of address – had strangely overpowered her. Again she felt that she loved him. The awareness came back suddenly, like a long-forgotten word. And she felt how much she was bound to him – by so many secret powers – and profoundly, how she could lose him. It was all so like a dream . . .

He talked on, his voice like a tender caress, his hand in her soft fingers now:

"I don't know if you have loved me – or at least as much as I now love *you*. Yes, love you with that decisive devotion – that all-consuming obliviousness to every trivial thing – that ultimate and most sacred love that can only give and never refuse. For I believe only in that sort of love that willingly sacrifices itself . . . Ah, but now it's all at an end. Even so, I have not loved you less . . ."

Erika was struck as if by a rapture. A soft shudder ran through her being. She knew only that she would lose him – and that she could *not*. And that she stood high above her life. . . Yes, all was so distant, far off. An evening stillness had settled upon the valleys: a mild solemnity. The city and its roar, and all that recalled reality, were so very far away. She felt herself high above it, in the sunny heights, high up and above all ugliness and mean-mindedness with the blissful might of self-sacrifice, the free and joyous love of the victim. No thoughts perplexed her anymore – no clever calculations. She felt only feeling – jubilant, overwhelming feeling like none she had ever known. The mood overpowered her and her will. And so she said softly and plainly:

"I have no one else in the world but you. And I want to make you happy."

All shame left her as she spoke. She just knew that, with one word, she could bring so much – so much happiness! And all she could see were his shining eyes and their grateful gleam.

And he bowed, and with silent reverence, kissed her lips.

"I have never doubted you."

They headed on down to the city, toward home.

By now that city was dark and weary of day. As they slowly made their way back, Erika felt as if she were climbing down from the crystalline snow of a blissful dream into hard and chill and pitiless life. Entering the fog-damp suburban lanes (filled with ugly, obtrusive noise and haze), she cast odd, anxious glances this way and that. A painful despair descended upon her. She felt hemmed in. The houses towered above her, all dark and smoky and bunched together – a dreary symbol of everyday drabness that bore down on her dream of destiny in order to crush it with thoughtless, threatening force.

She nearly flinched when, all at once, he began to address her with words of love. She'd nearly forgotten her promise! Those tender moments – how long ago they seemed! How strange to her now, in these dull, cramped surroundings, appeared that pledge teased out of her by the abrupt and impulsive might of a euphoric mood! She eyed him askance, and with care. His brow was furrowed powerfully. Round his mouth lay the calm of one self-assured. His whole expression was one of relentless male complacency. Nowhere could she find the mild wistfulness that typically bound his powers within a spell of a lovely harmony. There was only triumphant hardness now, with a brooding sensuality no doubt lying in wait. She slowly took in his look. Never before had he been so strange, so distant to her as he was now.

And suddenly she was afraid – with a crazed, unbridled fear! A thousand voices awoke in her – frightened voices that warned her, that made all kinds of noises and threatened to shout one another down. What would come now? She felt it only darkly, for she dared not think it through. All inside her rebelled now against that vow – that pledge snatched from her in a moment of weakness. Her hot shame burned like a wound. She had never been sensual; she felt that now in the depths of her heart. She had no desire for a man – just repugnance before this brutal, compelling force. Yes, now she felt only disgust. All darkened before her gaze, assuming a base and ugly significance: the tender pressure she felt on her arm; every chance stare she met in passing; two lovers who suddenly arose from the mist and then, as quickly, were lost again. The blood in her temples beat with a clear and furious agony.

All at once she felt a profound pain, and with it, disappointment quivered as if beneath chastening blows. What always happened would happen again: the sensual side of man would murder a girl's soft love and its holiest ardor. Joy, which had shimmered like evening clouds above the darkness, was shattered now. Night began to loom over her instead, black and brooding and full of threatening, sorrowful stillness and merciless silence . . .

Her feet could hardly go on. He was headed toward his apartment! The mere fact of this stunned her. She longed to say everything to him: how her love was different from his, how she'd made him the vow while under the spell of a mood she could put down to nervous emotions, and how all within her revolted against this promised tryst. But her words could find no voice – only grim and urgent black emotions that tortured her soul without setting it free. Dark, dire memories brushed up against her like looming black wings. One came again and again: an eerie yet really quite commonplace tale of a girl who'd gone to school with her – a girl who'd given herself to a man, and, when he'd gone off and left her, had given herself, out of rage or revenge (she didn't even know why, anymore) to another and then still others. And Erika shivered whenever she thought of this girl, through whose life love had passed like a dark thunderstorm. Her own wild reluctance was far, far more than the first bashfulness of an undefiled girl afraid in the face of the unknown event. It was, instead, the lovely weakness of a tender soul that shrinks in fear from everything loud and brutal and ugly in life.

Between the two of them, walking arm in arm, the chill and divisive silence remained. Gladly would she have freed herself, but her limbs seemed to have lost every means of movement; alone, her feet trudged on as if in a dream. And her thoughts grew more and more hectic: they shot here and there like glowing arrows that drilled into her brain like fine burning barbs. And over all that, ever more thickly, lay superimposed the mighty black cloud of dread and despairing surrender. Again and again, a prayer escaped her lips – a prayer that it all be over now; that she not have to think and feel anymore; that a great, dark, painless emptiness would come; that all would suddenly, sharply end, as when one wakes and is freed from an evil dream . . .

All at once he stopped.

She drew up with a start. They were standing in front of the house where he lived. For a moment, her heart stopped beating – grew quite rigid and calm. But then it started pounding again, swift and wild, with hammering angst and quickening speed.

He spoke a few words – sweet, loving words. Once more, for a moment or two, she almost would have had him again, he spoke with such warmth and fineness of feeling. But when he grasped her arm more firmly and, with gentle affection, pressed himself to her yielding body, the old dark dread returned again, and she felt more dazed and afraid than ever. She felt that her tongue would have to be freed so she could cry out and beg him to let her go. But her throat remained dumb and sealed. She let him lead her through the large, gloomy door half-consciously, with that agony of inevitability in her soul so profoundly deep it is no longer felt to be a misfortune.

They went up a dark spiral staircase. She felt the cold, musty scent of the cellar and saw the quivering yellow of gaslights, which shivered upon the chill air. She felt every step, every image glide past her, fleeting yet sharp, profoundly piercing yet fading within the next instant, like the sights one sees on the verge of falling asleep.

Now they stood in a hallway. She knew it: they were right at his door.

He stepped forward, letting go of her arm.

"Just a second, Erika. I'll get the light."

She heard his voice as he went in and lit a lamp. The moment gave her courage – the chance to come round. The feeling of dread came over her now like a fever chill, which cast off all her rigidity like a convulsion. And with lightning-fast strides she dashed back down the stairs – fast now, fast – without heeding the steps in her frenzied rush. She felt she could hear his voice from above, but she no longer wished to come to her senses, just ran and ran, without stopping. A wild dread had awakened in her (he might follow!) as well as the fear that she'd really like to go back to him. And not till she was several streets away and found herself in a strange neighborhood did she stop and, with a deep sigh, slowly begin to make her way home.

There are hours totally empty of incident, yet filled with a hidden destiny. They rise like dark, indifferent clouds that appear only to be lost again, and yet they remain stubborn, defiant. And like rising black smoke, they dissolve, grow more diffused and distant, until, at last, they drift without motion over one's life: shadows that cling, with a jealous inevitability, to all one's moments and raise their threatening fists again and again.

Erika lay on the sofa in her dark room in secret, pressed her head to the pillow, and wept. She could find no tears, but she felt them flowing in a stream inside her – hot, swelling, reproachful – and at times the sharp shudder of a sob ran over her body. With these moments of painful experience, with this first great disappointment, she felt a sorrow settle deep in her soul, which had opened itself up to it. In one respect, her heart did quiver with triumph to know her escape had been successful (and right in the nick of time), but this gave her no joy or satisfaction – only a dull, aching pain. For there are natures in whom every great event and outstanding occurrence strikes, with the soul's general tremor, the muffled string of a hidden sorrow and deep melancholy whose sound becomes so urgent and loud that all other moods are dissolved in it. And so it was with Erika Ewald. She mourned for her love, which had been so young and lovely, like a frolicking child immersed in life. And she burned with shame – a hot, scorching shame – to have fled like a dumb, helpless beast instead of simply being honest and speaking to him with a cool, sharp pride he'd have had to obey. And she thought of him and her love with a beatific pain, and a heated nervousness, and every image of it returned and reeled chaotically, yet no longer brightly and happily but shaded, darkened by the wistfulness of memory.

A door opened outside. She started sharply and unexpectedly, anxiously listening to every noise, and sought to interpret in each mild sound of excitement an unvoiced thought she did not quite dare to think.

Then her sister walked in.

Erika was confused. Why hadn't she thought of this – this obvious thing – that her sister would have to come in? Again she felt a curious sense of how strangely, enormously distant from her these people she lived with were.

Her sister began to ask her about her afternoon. Erika answered awkwardly, and noticing how unsure she was acting, she grew hard and unfair. She wouldn't be bothered with questions. Of what concern was she to anyone? Besides, she had a headache. And she wanted some peace and quiet.

Her sister did not reply – only left the room. And Erika felt how rude she had been. She pitied this silent, fated creature, who experienced nothing and asked for nothing, who owned nothing whatsoever in life, not even a rich and noble agony like her own.

That brought her back to her thoughts again. And these drew close, then were lost in the distance: cumbrous yet buoyant black crafts that struggled their way through a gloomy sea without a noise or even a murmur, without any aim and leaving no trace in their wake – only guided, propelled, by forces unknown and unseen. But their dim mood rippled on in her soul, only to be dissolved, after several dark and burdensome hours, within an exhaustion she yielded to without will.

The next day brought only anxious waiting. In secret, she waited for a message from his hand. She even longed for one with relentless reproaches and hard, angry words. For she wished to make an end to things, an end that would be considered the past.

Or maybe one would come with gentle words – understanding words that pierced into her soul – words that would lead her back into the round of those blissful hours from which she was now divided...

Yet the coming days – and all their mysterious developments – would only deny her these things. For no message came; no sign was placed between her and her torturing uncertainty. And she was still too much under the spell of her feelings and inner turmoil to know the answer to all her questions. Did her love still live? Had it already died? Would it be transformed into a new phase she could not yet foresee? She felt only unrest and confusion inside – a persistent tension that refused to be eased and that plunged her into ugly moods. With frayed nerves and headaches, she trudged through the hours, which grew more dreadful, more painful than ever, for they made her feel more acutely all that was false and discordant. And every noise irked her. The world outside grew unbearable: its loud insistence and haste, and even her own thoughts now, lost their gentle, agreeable dreaminess and acquired hard, cutting points. The tiniest thing concealed something hostile – some secret and spiteful intent that sought to hurt her. The whole world seemed only one big prison, some huge dungeon that sealed her in, its blinded windows blocking out light and hiding countless tools of torture.

And these days were unbearably long to her. They seemed not to want to end. She sat by her window and waited. Evening at least brought a little peace – with its gentle soothing of every contrast. When the sun slowly sank behind the roofs, when reflections quivered more vaguely and darkly, then all inside her grew milder, more restful. Then she felt all her thoughts and emotions might now become strangely different. Indeed, she felt new events and emotions standing before the gates of her life, calling out and craving admission. But these she did not consider. For she felt that these stirrings growing in her would only prove the final gasps, the fluttering death throes, of her fading love . . .

Two weeks passed with no word from him. All seemed over, forgotten. Her sadness and moodiness had not yet left her, but they were freed of their ugly irritableness; they had found refined and cerebral expression. The painful emotions had gently melted in wistful songs – melancholy melodies with deep and muted minor chords that sounded her lament. She played many evenings without thought, deviating slightly from a motif toward self-created combinations that more and more resembled the story of her anguish-filled love, which now sought to trickle back into the past.

She also began to read again. Those lovely old books, her favorites – exuding melancholy like the numbing fragrance of strange and dark, despondent blooms – grew dear to her once more. Once more to hand came Marie Grubbe, whose hard life destroyed a saintly, profoundly heartfelt love. Then the ill-fated Madame Bovary, who would not renounce the world and its joys and forego her simple bliss . . . Then the ineffably touching Marie Bashkirtsheff, to whom no great love had ever come, despite her rich, noble artist's heart and all its expectant longing . . . And Erika's anguished soul dove into these agonies of other women in order to lose and forget her own, though at times, a shock came over her, one that made fear and pride siblings. For words came to her eyes that held true for her own life – words whose sense of the burdens of fate she too could grasp. And now she felt that her own sad story declared no hatred of life and injustice; instead, it was painful only because she lacked the glad, strutting, laughing, and trivial way of the dancer who, quickly forgetting pain, springs clear of its dark but richly mysterious abyss. Now her loneliness alone still oppressed her. She was close to no one. An odd modesty, which lent a strangeness to her secret beauties and depths, had turned her away from all other girls who might have been friends. And she lacked the blissfully-trusting faith of the pious who speaks to a god and makes him the most discreet confessions. The pain that escaped her only flowed right back into her soul. And her ceaseless self-confiding, her endless self-analysis, left her at last with a vague exhaustion, a helpless fatigue, that made her too weary to wrestle with fate and its hidden forces.

Strange thoughts came to her when she looked from her window down onto the street. She saw people in wild confusion: rushing boys; cyclists jostling past; couples in love who ambled along, blissfully self-absorbed; fast-paced carriages with whizzing wheels – commonplace, everyday sights. But to her it was all so strange. How distant all of it looked to her! It all seemed from another world. For why did these creatures so hurry and push and storm their way past when their aims were so puny and base? As if those aims could provide something richer, more blessed, than that splendid peace in whose spell every passion and longing sleeps – that peace that dismisses every ill, peels away every ugly thing, in the way that a miracle-working spring, with its mild and secretly powerful waters, will skim off some irksome layer of film! So why all the struggles and conquests, then? Why the heated and never-exhausted yearning that none is allowed to escape?

So she thought at times, with a smile at life. For she little knew that the faith in this great peace is, in itself, a mere yearning as well – the most intimate, heartfelt craving – and one we may not fulfill for ourselves. Believing that she had conquered her love, she thought of it as of someone dead. Her memories of it assumed mild, appeasing hues. Forgotten episodes rose up again, and between reality and soft reveries, secret binding threads ran here and there and left her hopelessly confused. Her experience seemed to her now like some strange and lovely novel, some book one has read a long time ago, some story whose characters step forth and again speak their parts, some tale familiar and yet so distant – one whose every room, whose every scene, grows visible once again, as if lit by a light flaring up in one's mind and at once making all as it used to be. And her reveries led her to form ever new conclusions, which assumed a rapturous air in the evenings, though she found none right, for she wished for a mild and conciliatory end, one filled with grace and mature renunciation, a cool and friendly joining of hands, and fathomless understanding. All these romantic daydreams convinced her that now he waited for her as well – that he thought of her in a thousand heavenly agonies. And this belief by and by intensified to an adamant fact, allowing her trust to unfold with more and more sureness that all would still have to turn out well – that a soothing, conclusive consonance would have to redeem the strange, turbulent melody.

After long, long days she now risked, at times, a smile on her lips when she thought that her love, with its bitter wounds – all nurtured with cheerful and unsuspecting trust – soon would heal. She did not yet know that a deeply-rooted grief is like a brooding underground spring that burrows its way, in restless silence, through a mountain's rocks for a long, long time, in helpless rage, pounding and pounding at uncarved portals till it bursts through the wall and storms down the valley, not only with unrestrained joy, but with crushing waste and mighty ruin . . .

All would turn out quite differently from what she had dreamed. Love entered her life once more, but she had changed. No longer meek as a girl, with mild, blessing gifts, did love approach. It came, instead, like a storm in spring, like a passion-heated and craving woman whose lips are burning and who wears the deep-red rose of desire in her dark tangled hair. For the sensuality of women is not like that of men. With men, it glows from the very start, from the very first year of maturity, while for many girls it comes at first in a thousand shapes and disguises, creeps in as raptures and blissful reveries, as vanities and aesthetic pleasures. But the time comes when it throws off every mask, rips off the concealing disguise.

One day it all grew conscious to Erika. No noisy occasion forced it on her, and no coincidence. Maybe a tempting dream stirred it in her, maybe a book with strangely seductive force. Maybe a distant melody – one that she suddenly understood – or maybe an odd, suddenly flowering joy; it was never made clear to her. She just knew that she longed for him again, though not for tender words, no, not for quiet hours. No, she yearned for his powerful arms and heated lips, which had touched hers with burning longing once without understanding her dumb, pleading words. In vain did her maidenly modesty oppose this recognition. She struggled to think of those earlier days, when not the faintest breath of sultry sensuality trembled. She tried to deceive herself that this love – as she recalled it had been that evening, when with deepest repugnance she'd fled from his house – was long since dead and buried. But then there were nights when she felt her blood burn with desire – nights when she had to mash her glowing lips in her cool, cool pillows to keep from moaning and crying his name in the mute and pitiless night. Then she dared not deceive herself any longer, and the realization made her shudder.

Now she also knew that the vague restlessness she had felt in these days had not meant the death of her great and beautiful love. Instead, it had marked the gradual budding of this urgent force that now gnawed its way through her soul. And with an odd inhibition, she saw these tendencies, which had been so commonplace and simple (and yet which had issued forth new agonies) as the fiendish offspring of a dark providence. In the midst of this passion, which had come like a late autumn that hurls its fruits onto desolate, frost-covered fields, virginity's force was joined with the richness of unused days of youth that had never suffered from the insistent crises of the blood. A stormy, triumphant strength resided in her that brooked no opposition and no refusal, for it sprang over every obstacle and crushed every doubt.

She did not yet sense how weak she was in the face of this sudden desire. She just felt the craving inside her grow richly triumphant – just felt that she had to see him again, if only from afar, from a goodly distance, without being noticed, without his suspecting that she saw and longed for him. Once again, she brought out his photograph. Tucked away in a drawer, it had gathered dust. She gazed at it with a strange adoration. With ardent passion, she kissed the mouth. Then she held it before her once again and began to utter crazy words, violent words that she wished to say to him herself – words that begged him to pardon, forgive her for having behaved like a frightened child. And then she told him, in breathless phrases, of how she longed for him – of how she loved him infinitely – even more than he could comprehend. But all these ecstasies did not soothe her: she wanted to see him again in the flesh. For days she waited hour by hour, in vain, on a corner he tended to pass. Her impatience heightened so much that, at times – though quite timorously and uncertainly – a startling thought came to her: she should go to his rooms and apologize for how she had acted that night.

Then she saw a notice in the paper. He would be in a concert of his own! This was a sign, and it filled her with rapture. Now she had the best chance of seeing him again, and without his suspecting it. And slowly, terribly slowly, did the days pass – days dividing her from the scheduled, eagerly-wished-for evening.

She was one of the first in the grand concert hall, which shimmered with a thousand lights. A yearning unrest, which stretched the minutes to hours, had filled her and shivered all through her since dawn, when the realization that this was the day had torn the veil of sleep from her eyes. And then, every hour, she'd trod through dreamland, though all the little demands of her job were able to jolt her, over and over, out of her brooding expectancy and gently-soothing sense of longing. And when evening came, she took out her very best evening gown and put it on with the sure and ceremonial care that women alone possess when expecting the gaze of their loved ones.

She made her way to the hall an hour too early. Of course, she'd first planned a little walk, a brief rest for her nerves . . . But she'd hardly stepped out onto the street when she felt a dark force that urged her in one direction. Her measured steps grew quicker, more restless. All at once she stood at the building's broad steps almost with dismay, and ashamed of her lack of ease. Still, without thinking, she walked up and down there a little. Yet as the very first carriage rattled smugly past, she no longer strove to master her feelings but bravely entered the now-lit hall.

It was silent inside, and desolate. Its empty spaces invited sad reveries. But this did not last long. People pressed in more thickly. She saw no one distinctly – just felt the masses streaming in and, before her eyes, the trailing sashes of bright evening gowns, the dark confusion of bodies pushing, and all the many changing faces that seemed to her like masks. She was filled with impatient expectancy. In her eyes there was only one name, one wish, one word.

Then it started: the sharply rustling murmurs and movements, the restless preparations before the silence, the faint snap of opera glasses being opened, the rattling of lorgnons, the stirring and shuffling, that many-toned sound that was soon drowned in stormy applause. She sensed that he had entered, that he would come in now. And she closed her eyes. She knew she was much too weak to look at him silently now, no, not at this proud moment. She would have to rejoice or call out to him, to spring up or wave, but in any case do something foolish or rash. Her heart was hammering at her throat. She waited, waited, seeing it all with her eyes shut, as he stepped up, bowed, and now – yes, it had to be now – took hold of his bow. She waited till . . . At last! The first sound of his violin rose. It rose singing, like larks slowly rising, rejoicing, ascending from the fields to the sky. Then she looked up gently – quite carefully – as if into a dazzling, blinding light. And she felt a warm surge of blood as she saw him borne upwards, as it were, from this dark and silent sea through which the sparkling glasses, the searching gazes gleamed like shivering crests of foam. And she felt the utterly magical force of his playing once more. As the sounds rose and swelled, so her heart filled too. She felt laughter and weeping alike inside her: a turbulent flood of warm, trembling waves. She rejoiced in a joy produced by a thousand leaping shafts of sun that effervesced in her heart; she even felt it foam up in her throat – like the exultant shaft of a flashing, upwelling fountain. The music's mood seduced her once more; she was like one blind who does not know his way yet is willing to trust the loving hand of a stranger. And as the elation died down and the hall's dark sea, which had been charmed to sleep as it were, foamed up in wild and raging breakers of applause that threatened from every side, then a sharp pride rose up inside her. Her soul thrilled with the thought of his having desired her. All the ugly bitterness of those moments melted in this proud realization, in this triumphant hour of his artistry.

And so this hour became a profound and noisy feast for her longing and restless soul. She was all humility in that hour, one who merely yearns for and craves the pleasure of giving herself. In fact, she no longer thought of herself but only of him. She saw his yearning and fervor alone – no longer sounds and melodies – in the luring play of his violin.

Only one question gnawed at her: did he still think of her too? But then she received an answer that promised infinite bliss. In the wake of long storms of applause, he'd decided upon an encore. And he'd played but a few slow, plain rhythms when Erika turned pale. She listened and listened as if bewitched. She had recognized, with a shock, that song – the song of that first strange evening when he'd stammered it out in the twilight – just for her. And she saw it now as an homage. She felt that it sang of her, *to* her. She felt it a question that sought her out among everyone else in the hall; she saw its spirit soaring its way through the dark room to find her. A rash certainty swept her off into dreams of joy. She felt the song to be a confession that, yes, he had thought of her, and *only* of her. And happiness welled up within her. Again it was music that beguiled her – that lifted her high over every reality. She felt herself rising in flight, high over the others and free of the earth – just as when they'd stood together high over the city's distant roar – only higher still, much higher now than the world and fate, than every little misgiving and meanness . . . In the few moments of this encore, she sailed in blissful dreams above every limitation.

Not till the jubilant uproar that followed his encore did Erika wake from her dreams of flight. And in urgent haste, she rushed to the exit to wait for him. For now she also knew the sunny reply to her ultimate question, that question that had frightened her so and held her back – kept her from giving herself to him. For now it was obvious: yes, he still loved her–and even more ardently than before – with a lovelier, wilder, far greater love! For why else would he have sung, before all these people, this shining ode he'd created from and in honor of their love – this glorious song whose might had once overpowered and conquered her without her suspecting it? Today she would lay at his feet her giving affection – with all its carefully-guarded fruits – just so that he might, in gladness, lift her up . . .

She pressed on, with effort, till she'd passed through the exit to the spot where the artists tended to come down. There, people weren't bustling round with such frenzy; there, she could give herself up to her dreams (which were nestled in blissful certainty) without her being disturbed. Indeed, why hadn't she figured it out long ago – the fact that he could not forget her? This thought returned again and again to link itself with happy tidings for coming days. With a spirited smile she thought of how surprised he would be when soon, without suspecting, the wish that he must have dreamed of would all at once come true. And when . . .

She heard steps. They rang out – ever louder and closer. By instinct, she drew back into the dark.

Laughing and chatting, he came down the steps, tenderly leaning toward a lady friend in lace-trimmed dress: a pert little singer trilling some old operetta tune. Erika flinched. Then he noticed her. Instinctively, he reached for his hat, but halfway up let his hand idly sink. An angry, hurt, and sneering smile seemed to lurk on his lips, but he turned his head to one side. Then he led the little lady in the frilly dress to his carriage, helped her in and climbed in himself, without once turning back to Erika Ewald, who stood there alone with her love betrayed.

Such incidents, with their abrupt force, often wake a sorrow so dreadful and drastically deep that one no longer feels them as painful because, with their wild impact, one loses the aptitude for comprehension and conscious feeling. One only feels himself sinking, breathlessly, from dizzying heights – whistling down without will and resistance – to an abyss that one does not yet know, that one only senses to be coming closer, closer, and ever closer with every second, with every little fading unit of time that flies past in its whirling fall toward that terrible conclusion of which one only knows that it will be shattering.

Erika Ewald had already borne too many little griefs to be able to look a big thing like this calmly in the eye. To be sure, those little griefs had held within them a strange sort of rapture: they had led her to mild despondencies, to dreamy and wistful hours, to all those sweet little sadnesses out of which our poets create their deepest, most thoughtful verse. Yet while she had thought, at the time, that she had felt fate's mighty paw, it had really been only a rippling shadow of his threatening, outstretched hand. Having thought she had suffered life's darker forces, she had built, upon her awareness of this, a firm certainty that crumbled now, under reality's weight, like a child's toy in a sinewy fist.

And now, because of all that, her soul utterly lost its binding strengths. Life came to her like a hailstorm that shatters seeds and blooms to pieces. Before her lay only more gloom: an impenetrable, desolate, and far-reaching gloom that hid each path, blinded each prospect, and devoured without pity her echoing calls of fear. Inside her lay only more silence – mute and breathless: the silence of death. For much inside her had died, been killed, in a single moment . . . A bright, cheerful laugh that had not yet come to life but that wished, like a child, to seek the light . . . Then, with this, so much of that yearning desire of youth for acceptance, which the future promises and which senses joy and splendor right behind every portal that, now closed, might yet be opened at its wish . . . Then too, many feelings of trust in the world, including that self-sacrifice to all mankind, as well as that self-surrender to the greatness of nature, who uncovers feasts and miracles to her more faithful students alone . . . And lastly, a love that had once been endlessly rich because bathed in the dark, deep springs of pain and, through metamorphosis, transformed to perfection.

But new seed lay in this disappointment: a bitter hatred toward all around her, as well as a heated need for revenge that did not yet know how to make its way. Humiliation burned in her cheeks; her hands quivered as if, at every moment, they must fend off something with angry force. Though the weakness and shame had left her, the need to act grew ever more restless, urgent, distinct. A creature who'd let fate form and guide her now sought to confront and struggle with it.

And this aimless, unruly urge allowed her the pleasure of roaming the streets with no firm intent. Reality lay in the distance, far off. She had no thought as to where she was going; her legs grew sore with fatigue but pressed on with a frenzied excitement. In the attempt to wish away this pain that gave no rest, she wrapped herself more and more in her thoughts and sought, in all this rash running-around, somehow to forget him; yet she felt the pressure of tears that could not spring forth but that flowed and seethed inside her . . .

Once she stood before a bridge. Beneath her the waters swirled past, slow and black, with many bright, glittering points. So many stars – the bridge lamps' reflections – stared up at her like ripped-open eyes. And she heard, from somewhere, the faint, ceaseless babbling of currents breaking against a pier.

The sight hid the thoughts of death she felt. A shiver ran over her. She turned round. There was no one near – only black shadows darting here and there, a distant laugh at times, or the rattling of a carriage. But close by there was no one – none who could stop her. How easy, how quick it would be: one grip, one swing right over the rail, then just a few ugly moments of struggle below, down there in that silent darkness, then peace . . . rich and eternal peace, far from every reality: the soothing comfort of never having to wake again . . .

But then another thought! A bloated corpse dragged out of the water, an oddity that entertains; idle talk and chatter – sure, *that* no longer hurt! But one person could come to know about it and smile with the self-importance, the confidence of the victor . . . No! That could not be! Life wasn't exhausted, she felt; it still held the chance for one last thing, for one last desperate, groping act: revenge. And life was lovely even, and she had only lived falsely: she'd been good and trusting – mild and reticent – while one ought to be insensitive – greedy and sly like a beast of prey that is nurtured by alien forms of life.

A laugh rang out from her breast as she turned from the bridge – a laugh that made her shrink back, for she felt she did not really believe her unspoken words. Only the pain was true – that, and the glowing, seething hate, the blind obsession with revenge. How alien to herself she'd become! She no longer even knew who she *was* . . . How *worthless* she was! How bad!

She shivered. She wished to think of nothing now. She went deeper into the city again . . . Somewhere . . . Back home? . . . No – not back home! She thought of it with fear. There all was so gloomy and cramped and dull. There, memories lurked in every corner to point at her with fingers of spite. There she was all alone with her overwhelming pain. There he – the pain – could spread his thick black wing out wide to grab her and tightly, utterly tightly, squeeze her till all the life went out of her.

But where? Where? She racked her brains for an answer. She could ponder nothing else anymore; all her thought was focused on this one question.

A shadow was running beside her.

She didn't see it.

And she didn't note as it only drew closer and moved along beside her a while. Someone was walking next to her, an enlisted man who observed her face with eagerness in the moment she passed a streetlamp. Not till he politely spoke to her was she jolted suddenly from her thoughts. She needed a moment or two before she could grasp the situation she'd found herself in, and so she did not respond.

The enlisted man, a cavalryman – still very young and rather clumsy – would not be intimidated by her silence. He talked on in a halfway familiar fashion, and yet with a certain reserve. Obviously he was not quite sure as to whom he was actually dealing with; she'd not answered him; and indeed, she was so refined, so respectably dressed . . . But then, this way of walking alone, late at night . . . He couldn't quite figure her out, and understandably. But he talked on anyway, without concern.

Erika was silent. From instinct, she'd wanted to turn away, but her moments there at the bridge had brought on peculiar thoughts. To be sure, she now wanted to start a new life – no longer this dreamy sitting-around in a stupor with all that futile self-searching that had dealt her a thousand woes. Yes, a new life ought to begin for her: heated and bold and full of wild force. And then she thought of *him* again: a dreadful disgrace.

She'd get her revenge. She'd give herself to the first one who came along; because he'd scorned her, she'd taste the degradation right to the last, most bitter and maybe deadly dregs. In all her rashness, she seized and resolved on a plan for a cruel self-torture, a new disgrace to burn away and shed the old . . . And the chance had come right in time . . . A young man – the very first to come by – who knew and understood nothing of it . . . Yes, he'd be the one . . .

So all at once, she answered him. Oh yes, she would let him escort her. Yet her hasty kindness made him uncertain again. Who was this he'd approached? The way she spoke, the opera glass she carried (which she'd brought along from a concert), and her highly refined behavior – all this changed his glib manner toward her. This woman made him quite shy. He was really still only half a child, oddly decked out in a uniform (as if in the masquerade costume of a soldier), and up till now his adventures had been so humdrum as not to be thought adventures at all. For the very first time, he found himself next to a real enigma. For she would be rigid and silent for moments on end, ignoring all questions and walking as if in a dream, till at once, as if with a tenderness that was forced (but that, in a moment, she'd have forgotten), she laughed and joked with him, though at times he felt that her laughter had a false ring.

And the act of playing someone so thoughtless and obliging cost Erika no small effort, especially while a string of the craziest thoughts buzzed through her head. She knew what the outcome would be, and she wanted it; but again and again, a fear that she was betraying herself crept up. Yet the need for revenge, which could not be enacted positively, had found a compromise here, to be unfurled even if in a false direction, with the sword's blade turned against herself, for it – the need – was so overwhelming and strong that her feminine feelings rebelled against it in vain. Yes, there would – there should be – regrets . . . But just to know nothing of that humiliation . . . just to forget, even if in a rush of ecstasy – even if in a false, artificial, corrupting . . . just not to have to think any longer of *that* . . .

So she gladly accepted the young man's offer to take her into a restaurant, there to sit in a private room, although she vaguely sensed what that meant. But she didn't want to think of that. Just never to have to think of *that* . . .

At first came a little supper, of which she didn't eat much. But she did drink the wine, glass after glass, and in greedy haste, as if bewitched. It was not quite working for her yet. At times she viewed her whole situation with awful clarity. She observed the one sitting across from her, who was actually the right one – a better one she could not have wished for: a good fellow – red-cheeked, healthy, and earthy – a little vain and not too clever . . . who'd never suspect what might happen that night, what kind of role he was playing in a poor, tormented soul's life . . . who'd forget her in a day or two, and yet, who wanted her now . . .

In such reflective moments, her eyes would assume a dreamy expression, and her face reveal the gloomy shadow of an inner anguish. Then she would slowly enter the dream . . . Her fingers would tremble faintly . . . All would be forgotten, and the distant, submerged images would slowly, quite slowly, re-surface . . .

Then all at once a word or a touch would re-awake her. She would always need a moment or two to find her way back into everything, but then she would seize her wine glass again and empty it with one gulp. And then another, and still another, until she felt her arm sink heavily . . .

Meanwhile the boy had eased over beside her and was nestling rather closely. She noticed, but calmly joked on . . .

By and by she began to feel the effects of the wine. Her gaze grew unsure. She peered as if through the gloomy clouds of a far-streaming mist. And the tender, persuasive words she was hearing appeared to drift toward her quite blurred and forlorn, from somewhere very far off. Her tongue began to loll. She noted that, despite her attempts to remain clear-headed, her train of thought was growing confused. Something flashed and hummed and gleamed before her – something she could not resist. But along with the tiredness she felt – the fatigue that embraced her ever more closely and tenderly – came the sadness again. It was half the babbling, motiveless despondency of the drunkard and half the pain that had raged through her breast all evening and still had not made any headway. She was utterly lost in her sorrow – benumbed and lacking all feeling toward the world outside her – deaf to all words and soft caresses.

The boy could not quite grasp her behavior. How should he begin with her? He sensed that she was drunk, but even so, he wished she would rouse, ashamed as he was of the thought of taking advantage of her in her state. Yet her apathy was not to be stirred through persuasion but tender kisses. Rouse her he did, but when he tried to unbutton her blouse, something unexpected occurred – something that frightened him.

For the moment when he embraced her, she suddenly fell into his arms and began to cry uncontrollably. Hers was an infinitely terrible, pitiful sobbing – not at all the maudlin drone of a drunk – for in those sobs lurked a primal force like that of a beast of prey which has been confined in a cage for a year and suddenly, with delirious strength, has broken through. It was her deep and utterly saintly suffering and pain, which now had been darkly revealed to her and now, in those shuddering sobs, released. As Erika wept from deep in her breast, everything, all, now seemed to become good. For this glowing burden of tears, this smothering load of pent-up emotions, was wrenched from her in mighty, thundering heaves; she cried and cried; sharp shudders ran over her helplessly nestled body. But the hot fountains that were her eyes did not seem to want to run dry; they seemed to spill all the bitter sorrow that had slowly gathered in them like growing crystals that had hardened and would not melt. It was not her eyes that cried. Her whole slender, supple body shook beneath the hard heaves, and her heart shook right along with it.

In the face of this sudden and painful outburst, the young man was totally helpless. He tried to calm her – he stroked her soft braids softly and tenderly – but as her exertions only doubled, an odd and tender pity possessed him. Never in his life had he heard so much sobbing. This outrageous sorrow, of which he knew nothing, and whose enormity he could only guess at, instilled an attentive fear in him for this girl so helpless in his arms. It seemed a crime to touch her body, for it was too weak to muster the least resistance. By and by, it also occurred to him that he might be handling it all superbly, and his childlike joy in this strange adventure strengthened his will. He called for a carriage, and, finding out her address from her, escorted her right to her house, where with friendly and calming words, he took his leave.

When Erika found herself in her room again, the last remnant of drunkenness had passed. True, the events of the last few hours were blurred for her, yet she thought of them not with chagrin and fear but with peaceful calm. Those tears had glowed with the burden of her whole being, her whole youthful soul with all its grief, as well as its grand and oppressive love, its wild, burning disgrace, and its last, almost-fully-accomplished abasement.

She slowly undressed herself.

This is how it had to have happened. For there are people who are not born for love, for whom only the holy shudder of expectation blooms, too weak as they are to bear fulfillment's painful blessings.

Erika thought back over her life. She knew that love would no longer come to her now. She would not have the pleasure of searching for it, and the bitterness of renunciation had drawn near to her for the very last time.

For one moment still, she hesitated – in secret, inexplicable shame. Then she stood before her mirror and shed her very last item of clothing.

She was still young and beautiful. A resplendent freshness remained in her bloom-white flesh; her breasts trembled in gentle and almost childlike curves, rose and fell – faintly and tenderly, in a rhythmic play of blurring lines – from a wild excitement within. Her limbs shimmered with sleekness and strength. All about her, indeed, was ready-made to commence and raise up a freeing, empowering love – to give and take in a playful exchange, to work its way toward life's holiest height: creation's transfigured miracle. Should it all go unused and unfruitful, like the loveliness of a bloom that a wind blows away, a barren speck in the fertile field of humankind?

A mild and forgiving resignation came over her: the sovereignty of those who have passed through the greatest pain. And too, the thought that this flowering youth would have been for one, for one alone, one who had craved, then scorned her – even this last and most difficult thing to consider no longer made her resentful. Wistfully, she turned out the light and sought nothing more than the feeble joy of gentle dreams.

Those few weeks defined the life of Erika Ewald. All she had suffered stayed locked inside her, and the countless days that followed passed her by like an uncaring stranger. Her father died; her sister married a clerk; friends and relatives suffered good and bad luck; in Erika's hours alone fate was no longer permitted to enter. No more could life do her harm with its raging force, for she'd learned a deep truth: that the great and holy peace that surrounded her cannot be gained except through deeply resounding grief, that no joy exists for those who have not gone the way of sorrow. But this wisdom, which had estranged her from life, did not remain cold and unfruitful. The capacity for a giving, sacrificial love, which once had shaken her being with heated convulsions, now drew her toward the children she taught, her music students, to whom she spoke of fate and its malice as of a person they should beware. And so her months passed, day after day.

And when spring and then warm summer came to bless the land, then her evenings also overflowed too, and with a profound loveliness . . .

She was seated at her piano beside the open window. A fine and spicy fragrance, like that which early spring brings, drifted in from outdoors, and the big city's roar was as far away as the ocean that hurls its raging waves at the shore. The caged canary trilled its merriest tunes, and the neighbors' boys, with their crazed, lively games, could be heard outside on the walk. But when she began to play, all grew quiet out there; then faintly, quite faintly the door creaked open, and one boy's head, and then another, shoved itself in to listen with awe. And Erika teased out wistful melodies. Her slim white fingers seemed to shine like candles as her mild fantasies touched on faded memories.

And once, while she was playing so, a motif came to her that she couldn't recall. She played it again and again till at once, she discerned it: the folk tune – that wistful romantic air with which he'd begun his love song to her . . .

She let her fingers sink; and once more, she dreamed of the past. Her thoughts were wholly devoid of resentment and envy. Who could know? Maybe it *had* been best that she had not found, at the time . . . And yet (she was nearly ashamed of the thought) she'd like to have had a child by him, a lovely child with golden curls whom she would have rocked when she was alone, tended to when utterly lonely . . .

She smiled. What silly daydreams!

And again, her fingers felt for, sought, the forgotten love motif . . .

SPRING IN THE PRATER

A Romance

She stormed like a whirlwind to the door.

"Has my dress come yet?"

"No, my dear lady," the chambermaid said. "I don't think it will be here today."

"Of course not." She called out with a voice that quivered with a held-back sob. "I know that lazy one all too well. It's twelve right now, and at half past one, I ought to go down to the Prater for the derby. But I can't do a thing because of that fool. And all this lovely weather, too!"

In a wild fit of rage, she hurled her slender figure onto the narrow Persian divan, a sofa over-sumptuously adorned with drapes and fringes there in one nook of the tastelessly-furnished boudoir. Her whole being shook with anger to think that she couldn't take part in the derby, that grand event in which she, as a well-known lady and famous beauty, played such an important role. Hot tears streamed down between her slim and amply-ringed fingers.

She lay like that for a minute or two, then raised herself upright a bit so her hand could seize the little side table where she knew her praline bonbons would be. She popped one after another into her mouth, mechanically, and slowly let them melt away. And her heavy fatigue after a riotous night, the cool semi-darkness of the room, and her great agony all conspired to make her nod off slowly.

For roughly an hour, she dozed without dreaming, still half-awake. She was very pretty, even now when her eyes – which in all their happy unsettledness typically formed her strongest attraction – were shut. Without her finely-penciled brows imparting to her a worldly air, one might have held her for a sleepy child, so dainty and smoothly-flowing were her features. Sleep had eased away all the pain she had felt over lost delights.

Towards one o'clock, she awoke, surprised to find that she'd dozed off like that; and little by little, it all came back.

With fierce and nervous, repeated rings, she summoned the girl once more.

"Has my dress come?"

"No, my dear lady!"

"That wretched person! She knows full well that I need it. It's all up now, there's no way I can go."

And in agitation, she sprang up, paced her cramped boudoir a few times, then stuck her head out the window to see if her carriage had come.

It was there, of course. All would have been fine if that blasted tailor had just done her job! So she had to stay home. Bit by bit, she grew obsessed with the thought that she'd be the most miserable woman on earth.

Without knowing it, though, she almost took pleasure in being sad; she found an odd charm in chastising herself. And on this whim, she ordered the girl to dismiss the carriage – a command that the driver no doubt would gladly accept, given the loads of business he could do that day.

But she hardly saw the posh carriage trot away than she rued her command, and gladly would she have called him back had the thought of doing so not embarrassed her, for she lived in Vienna's noblest quarter, on the Graben.

So the game was up. She was under house arrest, like a soldier forbidden to desert his post.

Irritably, she paced the room. It was smothering here, in this stuffy boudoir so crammed with every last random thing: rubbish of the most irksome sort alongside exquisite works of art. And with it all came the stench of twenty perfumes. The reek of cigarette smoke clung to everything. For the very first time, it all struck her as disgusting. Even the yellow volumes of Prévost's novels held no allure for her today. She couldn't help thinking about the Prater – *her* Prater – and the joyful meadow where the Derby was held.

And all because she lacked the right outfit.

It was enough to make you cry. Indifferent to every thought, she leaned back in her leather armchair and tried to drift off to sleep again, to annihilate the afternoon. But it wouldn't work. Again and again, her eyelids opened and sought out light.

She went to the window again. The Graben shimmered hot in the sun. She gazed at the people rushing past. The sky was so blue, the air so warm, that her longing for freedom grew stronger, more urgent. Her wish for escape asserted itself more and more. She'd go to the Prater anyway! Indeed, she couldn't miss it! She could watch the procession at least, even if she couldn't take part. For that she'd need no fancy outfit. A simple dress was even better, for then no one would know who she was.

Her plan quickly took shape.

She opened her chest to select a dress. Shrill, dazzling, and lively hues glared up at her in a gaudy whirl; silk rustled beneath her hand as she sought for a choice, which wasn't that easy: nearly every item she owned had the firm intent of attracting attention – exactly what she now wished to avoid. After a lengthy search, she beamed like a child. She'd spotted, way down in one corner, quite dusty and crumpled up, a simple and almost shabby dress; and it wasn't the find alone that made her smile, but the former life this souvenir revived. She thought of the day she'd fled with her lover from her parents' home, all decked out in this little dress. She thought of the joy she had known with him. Then she thought of how she'd exchanged it all for the rich attire she'd worn as the lover first of one count, then another, and then . . . several more . . .

She didn't know why she still owned it. But it pleased her, and, when she'd put it on and eyed herself in the massive Victorian mirror, she had to laugh at herself, for she looked so girlish, so respectable – so childlike – in a bourgeois sort of way . . .

After some further scrambling, she found the hat that went with the dress. Then she tossed a laughing look at her mirror. A young bourgeois Fräulein in her Sunday best laughed back, then dashed away.

With that same laugh on her lips, she entered the street. At first she felt everyone could tell she was not what she feigned to be.

But the few people scurrying toward her in the noon heat had, for the most part, no time to observe her; and slowly she settled within her new role. With pensive face, she strolled on down the Rotenturmstrasse.

Bathed in the sun, all shimmered and shone. Sunday had turned brute objects and beasts into well-groomed and cheerful human beings. Everything flashed and gleamed and rejoiced. She eyed the jostling crowd (with which she typically never had contact) as if she were a "country cousin" who'd taken a carriage to town for a look, or so she said to herself.

Reaching the Praterstrasse, she saw that she had to take more care; for, right beside her, an admirer of hers rolled past in an elegant carriage. Her spirits welled up afresh. She could have plucked him by the ear had she wished, he came so close! But he took no notice of her, having leaned back in his genteel and negligent way. She laughed so loud that he turned around. Had she not dashed her handkerchief to her face, she likely would not have escaped him.

With a smile, she went on. Soon she was urged right into the swarms, the gaudy throngs, on their Sunday pilgrimage to Vienna's national shrine: the Prater, whose blond lanes span like lumber beams against the green of pathless meadows. Her gaiety went unnoticed amid the joyful mood of the mob, for the Sunday cheer and zest for nature made all forget the drudgery of the rest of the week.

She drifted along in the crowd like a single wave in the sea, bubbling, skipping along, and powerfully conscious of her joy.

She was glad that the tailor had forgotten her dress. For she felt *happy* here – free and filled with a bliss she hadn't known since she was a child – when she'd first come to know the Prater.

Her memories of those days now returned. And yet, because of her happy mood, they seemed laced with a bright gold hem. She thought of her first love again, but not with a sad defiance – no, not as something that makes one depressed – but as something good that one would so gladly live again, a love that one *gives*, that one does not sell . . .

Deep in her daydreams, she wandered on. The crowd's chatter became the dull roar of waves from which she could not discern a single sound. She was alone with herself and her thoughts, much more than she had ever been when lounging idly there on the narrow Persian divan in her room, blowing rings from her cigarette into the still and stuffy air.

Suddenly she looked up.

At first she did not know why. Somehow a dark feeling had cast a veil on her thoughts – one she could not disentangle. Glancing up now, she noticed two eyes fixed steadily on her – eyes that roused her from her dream. Though she hadn't looked for it, her feminine instinct read this stare correctly.

The stare issued forth from a pair of dark eyes that had their home in a youthful face that, given its childlike expression (and despite the imposing little beard) might be construed as pleasant. His clothes signified his student status; the flower tucked in a buttonhole – the national party's neat emblem – could only confirm this guess. The slouch hat shading obliquely the soft, standard features gave to this plain, almost commonplace head an ideal, poetic air.

Her first move was to knit her brows in scorn and proudly look away. What did this drab young fellow want from her? Indeed, she was no plain wench from the suburbs. She . . .

All at once she stopped, and her lively laugh again gleamed from her eyes. For a moment there, she'd seen herself as a lady of the world again, forgetting entirely the way she'd donned the disguise of a bourgeois maiden; and quite childishly now, she enjoyed the fact that the masquerade had succeeded so well.

Regarding the smile as an invitation, the young man sidled up closer, fixing her with a relentless gaze. In vain did he strive to give his features an air of confident manly triumph – one that his timid indecision destroyed again and again. And that was just what pleased her about him. For this restraint and reserve from the man's side was something alien to her. The ways of a child, which had not yet faded from this young man, indeed offered her, in her natural state, a new and unique sensation. Indeed, it proved a comedy of ceaseless humor to watch how the student pursed his lips a dozen times to speak, only to let them drop again and again, in the decisive moment, seized as he was by a coy anxiety and fear. She was forced to bite her own lips hard to keep from laughing right in his face.

To the good attributes of this young man, she could add that he wasn't blind. Indeed, he could clearly detect the telltale twitch round the delicate rims of her mouth, which only heightened his courage.

And quite politely yet unexpectedly, he blurted it out: might he have the pleasure of escorting her for a while? He gave no rationale for doing so – chiefly and simply because, despite his strained and intense reflection on the matter, he'd found no reason that might be of use.

And despite her own long years of practice, in the critical moment the question was posed, she surprised herself. Should she accept? Why not? She just couldn't allow herself to dwell on how it all would end. Now that she was already in costume, she'd play the role. Like some bourgeois girl, she'd walk in the Prater with her beau for once. It would even be amusing, perhaps?

So she decided to accept and told him thanks, but he might not wish to accompany her: he'd lose too much time. In this case the "yes" resided within the law of causality.

He understood this right away and kept on strolling at her side.

Soon a conversation was in full force.

He was a young and jovial student, having escaped high school by not many years; and he'd retained from those days a pretty good bit of his zest for life. Yet he'd experienced little. It's true that he'd loved with an infinite (if boyish) ardor; but the "adventure" most young people seek was all too rare for him, for he lacked aggressive temerity, the chief requirement for such escapades. For the most part, his love had been mired in the kind of longing that cautiously admires from afar and is lost in dreams and poetry.

She, by contrast, marveled to find what a chatterbox she'd abruptly become, not to mention the kinds of things she was starting to take an interest in, as well as how she'd suddenly lapsed back into her old-fashioned Viennese dialect, which she'd not spoken or even thought in for maybe the last five years. And to her it seemed that those five years of mad and elegant living had vanished without a trace, as if she were once again the yearning, life-thirsty kid from the suburbs who'd once so loved the Prater and all its magic.

Without having noticed, they'd slowly strayed from the path, away from the roaring stream of the crowds and into the Prater's spacious meadow, where spring was in fuller force.

The century-old chestnut trees, which rose like giants, were in full leaf now, of the deepest green. Their bloom-laden boughs stirred against one another like lovers' whispers, scattering fine-leafed balls of fluff like winter snow on the dark green grass, where gaudy blooms lay as if stitched into a strange pattern. A sweet, heavy scent welled up from the earth, flowing so softly one lost all *conscious* assurance of pleasure and felt instead a mere vague sense of something lovely, soporific, and sweet. And above the trees, the sky – so radiant, blue, and pure – formed a sapphire-studded dome. The sun spread her richest gold upon her immortal, miracle-filled, and unique creation: spring in the Prater.

Spring in the Prater!

The words took shape in the air. The two lovers felt the deep magic around them. The richness of buds in bloom tingled in them too. Arm in arm, they strolled through the meadows, beaming with joy. And in some children nearby, for whom this joy was still unfamiliar, a peculiar stirring had also awakened, making them leap and dance and rejoice. Their voices rang in the wind and far into the trees.

All were thrilled to be freed from toil for once. The Prater's spring crowned them like a halo.

The lovers had not yet noticed the way the magic had entered their own souls too. Yet bit by bit a certain intimacy had crept into their frivolous banter: an uninvited but welcome guest. Little by little, they'd become friends. This charming and merry girl, with her sovereign high spirits, seemed like a princess in disguise and filled the young man with delight. She was glad to win this fresh young lad, as well. And the comedy she'd begun with him had now grown a little serious, for along with the dress of those earlier days, she'd also donned the feeling again. She was filled with the longing, the bliss of that very first love . . .

She seemed to be living it all again now, and yet, for the very first time: this jesting awe, this hidden craving, this simple and silent bliss . . .

He'd lightly slid his arms under hers. She did not resist. She felt his warm breath on her hair as he told her a thousand things: of his youth, his exploits, of his name (it was Hans), of his life as a student, of how he liked her so awfully well. Half in earnest and half in jest, he made her a declaration of love that made her shudder with joy and glee. She'd heard hundreds of such professions, and maybe even in lovelier words; she'd also yielded to many. But none had made her cheeks blush so much as this simple, robust, yet heartfelt speech he now whispered into her ear, humming with soft and deep excitement. Like a dream one longs to live, the trembling words rang on. So did the quivering through her whole being – until she shivered with bliss. And she felt the pressure of his arms on her own grow tighter, as if in a wild but tender rapture.

Now they were deep in the spacious meadows empty of people. There the carriage's racket continued to hum, though with only a faint murmur now. They were almost alone. Only here and there, like white butterflies, did bright summer clothing flash through the green. Only here and there did a human voice drift its way toward them, strangely, as if in a deep and sun-weary sleep . . .

His voice alone did not tire of whispering a thousand loving words, each warmer and yet more bizarre than the next.

And she listened on in a daze, as one falling asleep hears distant music, unable to discern the separate notes – just the rhythmic, melodic components of sound.

And she did not resist when he drew her face close and kissed her – with a long and heartfelt kiss containing countless silent words of love.

And with this kiss, all her memories fled: it was like the first kiss of her life. And the game she had wanted to play with him was now rich with love and emotion. A deep affection had taken root that let her forget her whole past now. In this, she was like an actor who, at the moment of his highest skill, actually sees himself as the hero or king and no longer thinks of his craft.

She felt as if, by some miracle, she'd been given the chance to live her first love once more . . .

For the past few hours, they'd roamed arm in arm without aim in the sweet euphoria of tenderness. Now the sky began to glow. It burned with a rich, deep red that the treetops seized like dark black hands. The twilight's contours grew more blurred; the evening wind murmured in the leaves.

Hans and Lise (she usually went by "Lizzie," but her childhood name now seemed so dear, she'd told him to call her that) had re-traced their steps and were now approaching the people's Prater, the carnival area, which now announced itself from afar through its maze of sundry sounds.

A gaudy stream of people flowed past the stands, which gleamed with garish lights. Soldiers with their sweethearts, kids and older youths eager to see all the sights – all were swept inside the chaos of noise. Army bands and organ grinders, children's voices of every pitch, rifle cracks from the shooting stands, carnival barkers extolling their treasures – all fought to drown one another out. And all were massed together here with their most important advocates: their common cravings, which the stall- and innkeepers sought to subdue.

This was a brand-new Prater for Lise – or, better still, the land of her childhood, found again. The central lane with its carriages, its elegance and its *noblesse* – all this was still familiar to her; but now, like a child in a toy store, she reached for everything greedily, found it all irresistible. She'd grown lively and joyful again; her dreamy, lyrical mood had faded. The couple rollicked about in the sea of people like two little children set free.

At every stand they stopped to savor the calls of the booth's proprietors, who like raucous, monotonous market criers, lauded, in the most comical ways, contortionists, fortune tellers, and monsters, as well as the continent's largest lady, or the planet's smallest man. They joined in all the fun they could – had their fortunes told, rode the carousel, and laughed and romped so merrily that everyone watched them with awe.

Soon, Hans' stomach was growling. So they entered an inn that stood apart from the worst of the noise, which died down for them to a steady hum that by and by grew milder.

And here the two sat side by side. He told her dozens of jolly tales, inserting (though rather clumsily) one or two flattering comments in just to keep her good spirits up. He called her funny names that had her in stitches, uttered gibberish that made her shriek. And she, who usually preferred a distinguished and calm self-mastery, was zany as never before. Childhood stories she'd long forgotten came back to her. Lost images rose up, assuming their old funny shapes. She felt enchanted – so different, so *young*.

They chattered on a long time.

The dark veil of night had settled some time ago, but evening's sultriness lingered. The air felt vaguely burdened, as if under a heavy spell. Far off, sheet lightning flourished and twitched. Slowly the lamps went out, and people dispersed in different directions, each to his own abode.

Hans, too, got up.

"Come on, *Liserl*. Let's go."

She followed. They went arm in arm through the Prater, which stared at them darkly, mysteriously. The last gaudy lights flashed from the rustling trees like tigers' eyes.

They crossed the Praterstrasse, which gleamed in the moonlight. The street was nearly empty. Each step rang out on the cobblestones. Shadows flitted in timid haste beneath the lamps, which shone their sparse light indifferently.

They'd not talked of where they would go. But Hans had taken it upon himself to quietly lead the way. She sensed he was headed toward his room but didn't want to say so.

So, with few words, they went on. They crossed the bridge over the Danube. Then they crossed the Ring. Then they headed toward the eighth district, where the student quarters were . . . Then past the massive, sparkling stone buildings of the university, past city hall, and on toward cramped, shabby streets.

All at once he began to speak to her.

He spoke heated, glowing words. He uttered the cravings of youthful love in those fiery hues that only those moments of wildest longing lend. In his words lay a young life's whole wild yearning for pleasure and joy, for the richest aims of living. And his words waxed ever more fervent; like greedy flames, they flickered high. The whole essence of man had, in him, reached its peak. He pleaded to her like a beggar.

Her whole being quivered beneath his words.

Her ear filled with the blissful roar of wild melodies. She hardly understood what he said, but his urgency met her own soul's yearnings, which strove toward his.

Like a fairy-tale princess offering some rare, precious gift, she promised him what she'd given to hundreds simply for cash.

He stopped at a cramped old house and rang the bell, his eyes aglow with bliss.

It was all done quickly.

First a damp, dingy entrance they stepped through swiftly. Then many narrow and well-worn and winding stairs. She hardly noticed, though: with his powerful arms, he'd borne her up like a feather ball. The joyfully-expectant trembling of his hands flowed over into her own willing body, which rose ever higher, as in a dream. He stopped high up and opened a door to a little room: a dark, dingy space whose furnishings she could see only with some difficulty, for the moon's bright rays were scattered all over the torn white curtain adorning the narrow roof window.

Quite gently, he let her glide down – to embrace her more feverishly. Heated kisses ran through her veins. Her limbs, beneath his caresses, quivered. In whispers of longing, her words died away . . .

The room was cramped and dark, yes.

But his wings, stretched in silent and satisfied rest, spoke of an infinite joy. And the hot sun of love shone within the deep gloom . . .

It's still early. Not quite six.

Lizzie has just come home to her posh boudoir.

The first thing she does is tear open the windows – to take in the fresh morning air. For the sickly-sweet scent of perfume, which calls her back to her present life, disgusts her now. Once, she'd simply accepted this life with a blind and thoughtless fatalism. But yesterday's frolic, like a dream of youth, has descended upon her destiny and given her a sudden need for love.

Yet how can she go back to love again? Soon she will have to concentrate – to focus on one of her many admirers – yes, one, and then another. The thought positively fills her with fright.

And she dreads the day, which slowly brightens, grows more distinct.

But slowly she starts to reflect on the day before, which, like a stray shaft of sunlight, has drifted into a life otherwise dark and dim. And she forgets the day that must come.

On her lips now plays the smile of a child who wakes at dawn from a beautiful dream.

SCARLET FEVER

"When you go to Vienna," his friends back home had said, "rent a room in the Josefstadt." It would be near the university, they said, and all the students liked living there in that quiet, old-fashioned section that was, by tradition, their "stomping ground." So he'd set off right from the station, where for now he had left his luggage; and asking his way, he had trudged through the strange and noisy streets past the rushing hordes who, as if being hunted, darted here and there through the rain and gave him directions only begrudgingly.

The autumn weather was merciless. Sharp wet showers splashed down without cease, drummed in the gutters, soaked the last trembling leaves of the dun-colored trees, and tore the gloomy skies into millions of fine gray shreds. At times the wind hurled the rain like a sheet, flinging it onto the walls with a flutter, battering and shattering umbrellas. Soon all to be seen on the streets were the jolting carriages with their steaming horses, the shadows flung by those running past.

The young student went from house to house, climbing up and down several steps, feeling relief for a moment or two to be out of the nasty rain. He looked at several rooms, but none could please him. Maybe the rain and the chill gray light were to blame: they filled every room with a stagnant, stifling air. A faint sense of constriction rose up in him when he saw the squalor of several quarters: the filthy rooms he crept up to on crooked and clammy stairs. They all gave him, somehow, a first foreboding of the sorrows concealed behind the brows of those stooped little threadbare suburban abodes. He grew more and more discouraged in his search.

Yet at last he made his choice. He took a room in the upper part of the Josefstadt – not very far from the Gürtel – in a rather aged yet sturdy and massive house of old-fashioned bourgeois coziness. The room was plain and actually smaller than he had wished for, but the window looked onto a large courtyard – one of those old suburban ones where now a few trees stood, faintly rustling and shivering in the rain. This last timid patch of green, a forlorn reminder of the gardens of home, appealed to him; and then, in the hallway, when the clock struck, a canary began to trill in its casing, and he did not tire of its coloratura for as long as he was inspecting the room. This seemed a good omen to him; and he also liked the landlady, a careworn, elderly woman – a civil servant's widow, she said. She herself occupied a mere wretched closet with her little daughter beside the room of another student, whose presence the calling card on the entrance door revealed.

In the few hours left till evening, he urgently wished to see some of the strange old city he'd dreamed about for years. But the chill and wind-whipped rain soon banished that wish. He entered a coffee house and sat a long time, his mind a blank as he watched the white billiard ball chase the red. Alone amid the chatter of so many strangers, he struggled to beat down the bitter feelings of disappointment that rose to his throat and sought release. Once again he tried to roam the streets, but the rain was too obstinate. Thoroughly soaked and dripping wet, he slipped into an inn for a quick, joyless supper before he headed back home.

Home . . . He stood in the room he now called "home" and looked around. A few things devoid of charm or life, and no real sense of belonging together, leaned against one another as if abandoned: two old wardrobes, tilting forward and heaving loud sighs whenever you stepped too close; a bed with threadbare blankets; a lamp hovering gloomily in the dark; and a frail "Old-Vienna"-style stove for heat. In between, a few color photos and prints – bleached things that hung beside one another yet lacked any clear connection. Strangers' faces had stared from their frames for years now, maybe, with no one having the least idea who they were. And then, from the uneven floorboards, a chill rose up, the same draft the window shut out poorly, with a restless clatter, when the wind tossed the rain against the panes.

He stood there and shivered, a stranger amid all this secondhand junk. Who'd slept here in this bed? Who'd rested here in this armchair? Who'd gazed into the mirror from which his own pale child's face now peered with an anxious look – almost, indeed, with a sob? Nothing here recalled his own life and past. He felt the chill deep down in his blood.

Should he go to bed? It was just nine o'clock. He was sleeping under a strange roof now for the very first time. At home they were all probably still at supper, having a nice quiet chat at the table, their faces lit up by the lamp's golden glow. Soon, he knew, his sister would go to the piano to play some wistful sonata or laughing waltz that he had requested . . . But where was *he*, who usually stood in the shadows beside that piano and dreamed to the sounds till she stood up and slowly bade him good-night?

No, he could not sleep yet. He took out the few belongings in his suitcase, which he had retrieved. All his things had been carefully packed. Disturbing their neat arrangement, he thought of the loving hands that had done this for him. Among his books, he was happily shocked to find a picture of his sister with a hearty greeting written upon it. She must have slipped it there in secret . . . He gazed at her bright, laughing face for quite a while, then placed the picture on the writing desk where he could see it and might be comforted by it. But the smile in the picture seemed to grow ever murkier – as if his sister were with him here in the dark, feeling sad right along with him. He hardly dared to look at it anymore, so dark did it already seem to him.

Should he leave this depressing and comfortless little dungeon yet again? Stepping up to the window, he saw the rain falling restlessly. A drop would settle on one of the cloudy panes and remain poised there till another joined it; then both would slide down like tears on a child's glistening cheeks. From every side, ever new ones came and slid down again, as if a whole world out there were shedding its sadness in millions of tears. He stood there for maybe half an hour. The steady and ceaseless fall of rain, the trees' inexplicable, plaintive music – both joined to express the grief deep in his heart. A wild sadness assailed him that screamed for tears.

He felt he would burst. Was this his first night in Vienna? How often he'd lived it out in advance – in dreams, in talks with his sister and friends. He'd thought of nothing specific – only of something wild and bright: a sort of rampage through the glittering streets – onward, yes, ever onward – as if in the morning none of the gleam would be left – as if, in only the first few hours, he'd have seen and lived it all. Laughing and chatting, he'd seen himself, heart pounding, singing his lungs out, and twirling his hat up into the night . . . Yet now he stood there before the blind panes, shivering and all alone – just stood there and stared while the drops ran down, two and now three and then two again – stared as they sculpted faint tracks in the glass; and he squeezed his eyelids shut so his own tears wouldn't fall and spill on his shivering hands.

For years, he'd been longing for *this*?

How slowly the time went by . . . The hand on the old clock's wooden casing crept forward quite imperceptibly. He felt more and more threatened by fears of the night. Inexplicable childish worries besieged him – a dread of being all alone, in this strange, dark room – as well as a furious longing for home he could no longer silence. He was all alone in this great big city – alone with a million beating hearts. Not a soul said a thing to him. Not a single soul had even heard of him or looked at him here, with the rain splashing down and mocking his tears and scorning his sobs. He felt ashamed to be acting like a child, yet how could he save himself from this fear that loomed in the dark and peered at him as if with eyes of pitiless steel? He had never longed to talk to someone as much as he did now.

The door next to his rattled open and then slammed shut. He sprang up and listened. A rough yet competent voice on the other side of the wall was humming a stanza from an old fraternity song. Then a matchstick crackled and whirred, and he heard the person fiddling round with the obviously lit-up lamp. That could only be his neighbor: a student of law, the landlady had said, who was studying for his exams. He breathed a sigh of relief, feeling his sense of abandonment calm down a moment. From the other room creaked the hard, heavy steps of someone who was pacing the wooden floor. The song rang more and more clearly; and all at once he felt ashamed of himself for standing there, trembling and eavesdropping, so he slunk back to the table, as if afraid the other could see him through the wall.

Now the voice grew silent. The pacing subsided. Evidently his neighbor had sat down. And now the rain with its whistling sound began to harangue him again, and his loneliness with all its angst peered out at him from the dark.

He felt he would suffocate here in this cramped little space. He could not stay alone here now – oh no. He sat up and paused till his cheeks were no longer red from his lying there, tested his voice by clearing his throat, then crept his way out and over to his neighbor's, where he stood for a moment or so before he could get up the nerve to tap rather timidly on the strange door.

A silence – apparently one of astonishment – followed; then a bright "come in" rang out.

He opened the door. Blue smoke streamed toward him. The cramped little room was quite stuffy; and at first every object within it was blurred in the thick rolling drafts of fog. He entered hesitantly. His neighbor, who eyed him with amazement, stood tall and upright, with no hint of being embarrassed, even though he had shed his waistcoat and vest and his shirt was half open, exposing a broad and hairy chest. His shoes lay sprawled here and there on the floor. His body – strong and ripe and crude – looked more like a laborer's than a student's as he stood there, a short shag pipe in his mouth, blasting strong puffs of smoke toward the door.

The one who'd entered now stammered a word or two.

"I've just moved in today and would like to introduce myself as your neighbor."

The other clicked his heels together mechanically.

"Pleased to meet you. Schramek. Student of law."

Hastily now, the visitor – to make amends for his own omission – provided his name.

"Berthold Berger."

Schramek sized him up with a look. "You're in your first term here?"

Berger answered in the affirmative and right away added that it was his first day here in Vienna.

"You're studying law, of course. Everyone these days studies law."

"No, I'll be enrolled in the school of medicine."

"So, bravo, finally one of those . . . But please, sit down a while."

The invitation was a hearty one.

"You'll have a cigarette, my good colleague?"

"Thanks, but I don't smoke."

"Well, that's all right. You non-smokers are a dying breed. A cognac then. A good one."

"Thank you, no . . . thanks very much."

Schramek laughed and hunched his shoulders.

"My dear colleague, don't be angry, but I sense that you're a softie, as they say. No cognac, not smoking – that's very suspicious."

Berger blushed. He was ashamed to have been so awkward, showing his clumsiness right off; but he felt that a tardy acceptance would have been even more laughable. In order to say something, he apologized for the nighttime visit again. Yet Schramek did not let him finish but stopped him hard with a couple of questions. They were nearly compatriots – one from German Bohemia, the other from Moravia – and they soon found a common bond.

Their conversation grew lively. Schramek talked of his exams, his contacts, and all the hundreds of stupid things that students seem so inclined to discuss. A highly-charged heartiness marked his storytelling: a noisy cheerfulness, and a self-assured, almost arrogant sense of his own experience. He clearly relished impressing a fellow fresh from the sticks. And in this he succeeded more than he knew. Berger listened to him with keen curiosity, for Schramek seemed to be announcing it: the new life awaiting him here in Vienna.

Schramek's brash and dashing talk pleased him. And as Schramek shot fat blue cones of smoke from his face, Berger seized on each little bit of trivia, for this was the first real student he'd met, and having none to compare him with, he took him for the best.

And he would have liked to tell Schramek a thing or two, but all that he had to say of home seemed humdrum beside these dazzling new things. So dull and flat, all his high school jokes and provincial life! All his own thoughts and words till now seemed just to belong to childhood, and here was the onset of manliness.

Taking no note of his silence, Schramek savored richly the shy and adoring gaze of the novice. At his request, Berger traced with careful hand the three dueling scars that carved a sharp red track over Schramek's close-cropped skull; he marveled at Schramek's account of card games and duels. He grew anxious yet eager to think he himself would soon be eye to eye with an adversary, and he begged Schramek to let him hold, for just a moment, the saber kept in one corner. It was, to be sure, a painful feeling when he found he could raise it only with arduous strain: he marked yet again how weak and childlike and lean his arms still were, and he felt, with a sudden envy, the distinction between himself and these robust and stocky fraternity boys. How incredible it seemed that one could twirl such a saber through the air with a whistling sound, strike through the parry with all one's might, and tear right into a stranger's face, just so. To him all these everyday things seemed just as colossal and admirable as grand and worthwhile deeds, and the shy adoration with which he spoke of them only made Schramek more loquacious and intimate. Schramek spoke to him as to a friend, unfurling for him the whole gaudy tapestry of his life, which had hardly been that of an ideal student, but which Berger idolized. He had found the harbinger of his new life.

At last, around midnight, they said their good-byes. Schramek warmly shook Berger's hand, slapped him on the shoulder, and assured him, with that spontaneous feeling of friendship one knows only in those years, that he was "quite a dear fellow," which infinitely pleased the enchanted young man.

Quite drunk from all these impressions, he went back to his room, which no longer seemed so lonely and gloomy, even if the rain still splattered at the window and chill air flowed from each crack. His heart was full of strange sparkling things, and he felt it indescribable luck to have found a friend on the very first day. To be sure, a faint wistfulness interfered as he felt how weak, how childish – how very school-boyish – he was beside this fellow who stood with both feet firm on the ground of life. He'd always been the weakest, sickliest, most pampered of all his comrades – always behind in games and high spirits – but not till tonight had he felt it so painfully. Could he ever become like Schramek: hard and strong and free? A wild longing came over him. To have muscles, to talk so dashingly – to grab hold of life firmly and not have to keep making deals with it somehow – could he ever be like that? With mistrust, he looked in the mirror at his bashful, slim, and beardless child's face. Again it occurred to him that he'd hardly been able to lift the saber, his arm was so weak. He also recalled that for nearly two hours he'd wept like a child, and only because it was dark and cold and he'd no one near. A fear hovered faintly above him: how would it be with him, the weak one, the childish one in this strange city, in this new life, where one needed courage, spirit, and strength? No – with effort, he roused himself – he'd struggle until he was fully worthy, strong and forceful, like his friend. He'd learn it all: the swerving walk; the bright and brash way of talking. He'd tone up his muscles and be a man.

Sadness and joy, despair and hope – all meshed in his mind. His reveries waxed more and more confused. Not till the lamp began to smoke did he see it was getting late, so he hurried to bed. Outside, the relentless September rain kept drumming down.

That was Berthold Berger's first day in Vienna.

And so it went the next time, as well: an impure mixture of sadness and joy, hope and despair – a fuzzy feeling with ever a sense of the unfamiliar and strange. The great and unexpected new thing he *had* expected – from Vienna, his freedom, his time as a student – would not present itself.

True, there were beautiful things. Schönbrunn in the gentle gleam of September . . . He loved its golden lanes, the way they slowly rose to splendor, the sweeping and spacious look they commanded over the noble garden and royal palace. He loved the theater with its plays, its intriguing mingling of so many beautiful people. He loved the city's elegant celebrations and fests and the way the streets, at times, were thronged with so many lovely faces and gleamed with a thousand enticements and promises. But these were always only just sights to behold and never things he could penetrate. They made him feel as if he were only greedily reading a book. Never once did he feel the immediacy of a real conversation or incident.

His one attempt to enter this brand new world was made in the first few days. He had relatives in Vienna: refined and genteel people who asked him over for supper. They were cousins of right about his age, and very kind to him. But he felt too strongly that, when they invited him, they were only fulfilling an obligation; he felt that, at his approach, they suppressed a pitying smile. He felt ashamed of his shy provincial ways, which must have looked pathetic beside their suave self-assurance. He was glad when he could take his leave. And he never went there again.

So everything urged him back to the friendship of that first evening, to which he gave himself with all the passion of one still half a child. He entrusted himself completely to this strong and healthy fellow, who took his exuberant love quite willingly and returned it with that ever-ready heartiness of inwardly indifferent people. After only a couple of days, Schramek joyfully offered the option of using the familiar "Du" to the blushing Berger, who would have tried it out only awkwardly and timidly, and only after a much longer time, so great was his awe for his friend, whom he thought superior.

Often, when they went walking together, he would secretly eye his friend to learn the other's certain and swaggering stride, as well as the casual way he would point out every girl they passed. The way he twirled his cane on the street as if he were fencing with it, the constant reek of tobacco in his clothes, the loud and challenging talk in the local bars, then the sometimes stupid jokes – even these nasty little habits pleased him. He could listen for hours while Schramek told the most trivial stories of card games, parties, and girls. Without his being able to help it, all these things, which did not concern him, nonetheless excited him, grew important to him; they seemed to be the real, true life; and he burned with longing to experience them. In secret, he hoped that Schramek would, for once, draw him into such adventures, but the other had a peculiar way of shutting him out of important affairs. Schramek must have felt that his childish and beardless face was not impressive enough, for he seldom took him along when he went in his fraternity colors, and they met each other most often only in the coffee house or in Schramek's room. And the initiative always had to be Berger's.

Berger had noticed that early on, and it clung to him like a secret grief. In his friendship for Schramek, as in every friendship of the very young, there was something of love, its impetuous passion, as well as a mild jealousy. A certain bitterness, to which he of course did not dare give expression, took hold of him when he noticed that Schramek was just as warm, and even more so, with quite naïve and indifferent boys whom he had just met. And he felt that, as much as he'd given of himself to the other in the few weeks now since he had met Schramek, he'd not come one step closer to him than he had on that very first night. It frustrated Berger that Schramek never gave more – nor less – than a hearty greeting, that he hardly listened when Berger said something about himself, that he showed not a whit of interest in *his* affairs (no, never, ever as much as *he* showed in Schramek's), that he seized every chance he could to talk of himself.

And then, the most bitter thing: with every word, Berger felt that Schramek did not really take him seriously – especially in what he called him! Instead of Berthold, as in the beginning, he now always called him "Bubi." Yes, that sounded warm and dear, but it gave him pain again and again. For it pierced him right in the spot that had bled in him for years, unhealed: the fact that he was always seen as only a child. For years now, the thought had burned in him. At school, he had seemed like a girl to everyone – so spoiled and shy. And now, when he ought to be a man, he just looked like a boy and had all these nervous and timid ways! People never believed that he was a medical student! Of course, he was not quite eighteen yet, but he must have looked much younger. Again and again, he sensed that his outward appearance alone was what made Schramek embarrassed to show him before his comrades.

One evening, he won full assurance of this. He'd been roaming the city for quite a while and once again, in the raging streets, he had felt that all-consuming loneliness, so he went inside for a chat with Schramek, who greeted him warmly from the sofa, although without standing up.

On the table lay Schramek's fraternity cap. It seemed to glow red as fire, and it stung Berger in the eye. That was his fondest, most secret wish – for Schramek to bring him into his club. For there he'd have all he so painfully missed: intimate friends, a home . . . There he could be as he wished to be: strong and manly – one of the guys. For weeks he had waited for words from Schramek – for some sort of invitation. He'd made several furtive and careful hints that Schramek had only ignored. And now this red cap burned his eyes; it seemed to flit like a living flame; it flickered and glowed and absorbed all his thoughts. He felt compelled to bring up the subject.

"Did you go to your club this morning?"

"Of course," said Schramek – with instant interest. "It all got colossally rowdy. Three new devils were taken in – really quite capital, solid lads. Of course, I'll have to act as one's second. It'll all be colossally fine. This Thursday, don't wake me till two: we won't get home till dawn."

"Yes," said Berger. "I am sure it will all be colossal fun."

He waited. Schramek said nothing. Why should he go on talking? But the cap on the table – red, fiery red – enticed him ... It gleamed like blood.

"Say ... Couldn't you take me sometime ... along with you, of course ... I'd like to see it all sometime, you know."

"Oh, sure. Come over sometime. Not tomorrow, of course. But I'll show it all to you sometime – naturally, as a guest. Bubi, I know you won't like it at all; it can get pretty crazy there, but if you want ..."

Berger felt something rise in his throat. This cap, this alluring red dream – all at once he saw it as if through mist. Were those tears before his eyes? He swallowed, then pressed on, wildly:

"Why shouldn't I like it? What do you take me for? Am I just a kid?"

There must have been something in his voice, in his tone; for Schramek at once sprang up and came over and gave him a gentle pat on the shoulder.

"Now, Bubi, you mustn't be angry. I didn't mean it that way. But from what I know of you, I really don't think you'd be quite suited. You're too refined, too upright – too *decent*. You'd have to be a pretty tough dude to win the others' respect – even if just for the drinking. Can you see yourself boozing or fighting the way they are now, every minute, in the meeting hall? Now, isn't it true? It's no tragedy, really; but you just wouldn't fit."

No. He wouldn't fit. There Schramek was right, he felt. But where *would* he fit? Why in the world had he ever been born? Should he be angry at Schramek for speaking so frankly – angry, or grateful instead?

Schramek, of course, after a minute or two, had forgotten all about it. Now he was blabbing away again. Yet Berger was eaten up more and more by the thought that they all thought him despicable. The red cap seemed to glare at him. He made no attempt to stay any longer and went on back to his room for the night, where he sat up late – till long after midnight –

his hands lying limp on the table while he stared motionless in the glow of the lamp.

The next day Berthold Berger did something stupid. He had not slept a wink the whole night, he had been so perturbed. To think that Schramek held him for a coward and a kid! He'd prove to them all that he didn't lack courage. He'd pick a fight and provoke a duel – to show them he wasn't afraid.

In this, he did not succeed . . .

He had learned from talking to Schramek how these things got started. Every day in the little cellar room of the nearby inn where he took his meals, a couple of the fraternity boys sat right across from him. It wasn't hard to start something with them, for their every thought revolved around these so-called "insults to one's honor." They never spoke of anything else.

In passing their table, he brushed against it on purpose, overturning a chair. Then he walked calmly on – without an apology. His heart pounded in his breast.

Already, behind him, rang a sharp and threatening voice.

"Can't you pay attention?"

"Lecture somebody else!" Berger shouted back.

"What cheek!"

He then turned round and demanded the other's card, handing the fellow his own. He was glad that his hand was not trembling. The whole thing had happened in a heartbeat. As he proudly walked out, he heard laughs and a merry retort:

"What a fruitcake!"

Which punctured his pride somewhat. But he stormed back home anyway. With glowing cheeks, and a joyful stammer, he pounced on Schramek, who only stood there while he told him all (omitting the final putdown, of course, as well as the fact that he'd upset the chair on purpose). Of course, Schramek would have to be his second.

He'd hoped that Schramek would slap his shoulder and praise him for being such a sterling chap. But Schramek only stared at the calling card pensively, whistled through his teeth and said, with annoyance:

"So you've just taken your pick! A beefy fencer like him. One of our best. Who'd hack you right in two."

Berger did not flinch. That he would be cut up a bit was understandable, given that he'd never wielded a saber before in his life. He thrilled at the thought of a gash on his face. Then there would be no more question. Then they would call him a man. But what disturbed him was Schramek's reaction. His friend just paced up and down and muttered:

"It won't be easy. He called you impudent, right?"

At last Schramek stopped and said to Berger:

"I'm going down to the hall right now to look for a second for you. Don't worry: I'll take care of it."

Berger was actually unconcerned. He felt a wild and almost effusive joy to be handled officially, for the first time now, as a student, a man. Now he had his own special "incident"! All at once he almost felt strength in his limbs. He took up the saber and twirled it. Ecstatic, he slashed the air hard with it. All afternoon, he paced up and down, dreaming fiercely of the duel. The certainty that he'd be defeated gave him not the slightest pain. On the contrary: he'd show his friend and all the rest that he wasn't afraid, that he'd stand his ground while blood streamed over his face and his eyes. Why, he wouldn't budge even when they struggled to wrench him away! Then they'd offer the red cap to him, they would.

He worked himself up quite a bit, and at seven that evening, when Schramek returned, he sprang up with glee to greet him.

Schramek was quite cheerful, too.

"Now, then, Bubi. All is well. Everything's fine."

"When are we on for?"

"But Bubi, we're not going to let you fence with them. The whole thing's settled, of course."

Berger went deathly pale. His hands trembled. A fury seized him that nearly brought him to tears. He could have struck Schramek right in the face as the other said:

"It wasn't easy, of course. Next time, be careful! It doesn't always turn out so well!"

Berger struggled in vain for words. But the disappointment was much too great. Finally, swallowing a sob, he said:

"I thank you in any case. But you've done me no favors here."

And with that, he left.

Schramek watched him go, with a baffled look. But he merely chalked this behavior up to the over-eagerness of a beginner and gave the matter no further thought.

Berger began to look around. His life at last sought firmer footing. He'd been there for weeks and had gotten no farther along than he'd been on his very first day. Like clouds that flutter and, one by one, slowly sail away, his childhood's dream-rich promises were fading, dispersing now in mist. Was this really the great Vienna, that glorious city, his dream for years, yearned for ever since he'd first scrawled its name with stiff, clumsy letters? Back then he'd thought of it all as maybe only a few more houses and bigger, gaudier merry-go-rounds than the one in their market square when the church fair was held. Then bit by bit, he'd slowly borrowed the hues of the many books. He'd let attractive, desirable women stroll coquettishly down its streets. He'd named the houses and peopled them with bold exploits: nights filled with zany camaraderie and all that applied to the dizzying whirl we call youth and life.

And what was there now? One room, cramped and bare, that he fled from each morning to spend a few hours in sweaty study halls. An inn where he quickly gulped down his food. A coffee house where he killed time staring at newspapers and people. An aimless roaming up and down noisy streets till he was so tired that he trudged back home to that cramped, bare room.

Once or twice he did go to the theater. But it was always a bitter occurrence. For when he stood up there in the gallery, packed in with the hordes who knew nothing of him; when he gazed down into the pit and the boxes; when he saw all the gentlemen, posh and adroit; when he saw the ladies, alluring in all their jewelry and low-cut gowns – when he saw them greet one another and laugh with glee – then he saw the way they all "belonged." The books had not lied. Here was the truth behind his fantasies, the reality behind those dreams he'd begun to doubt because they had not been fulfilled. Here was the world that all the silent houses normally hid. Here was adventure, experience, fate. Here, in endless shafts, it drifted down: life's gold. But *he* just stood there and gaped at it all and could not enter in. Yes, his childhood thoughts had been right: the gaudy and shimmering carousel was grander here than the one at home; its music was louder and more resounding, its flourish far more breathtaking and wild. But he only stood and watched as it passed. He could find no way onto it.

It wasn't shyness alone that held him back. Lack of money kept his hands tied, as well. What they sent from home was too little for him. It kept him dangling right over the cliff of want, proving only enough for this silent and simple, drab sort of life. It never sufficed for that lavish exuberance to which every youth is inclined. To be sure, he would not have known what to do with money. But just knowing what was denied to him, all that he vaguely felt lovely, exciting (charging wildly through the Prater in a carriage, or whiling away the night somewhere, imbibing champagne in some elegant bar with gorgeous women and friends – throwing money *away* for once, on a crazy whim, without having to pay for the chance later on) – just knowing this filled him with shame. Those raucous student free-for-alls in smoky locals disgusted him . . . The burning longing to salvage, just once, from the barren rut of his daily routine, some vital feeling in some outrageous spree, some mad extravagance in which some of the grand pulse of life, of youth's unrestrained and natural rhythms, still resonated – this longing grew wilder and wilder.

But all of this was denied to him, and at each day's end came the bleak return to that cramped, dark room where the shadows loomed as if they'd been scattered by evil hands, where the mirror glowered as if iced over, and where, at night, he feared waking up in the morning and where, in the morning, he dreaded the long and sleepy and empty and tedious trek toward night . . .

In these days he grew extremely eager, with a certain sort of desperation, to give himself to his studies. He was the first in the labs and the lecture halls, the very last to leave; he labored with a dull greed, and without regard for his classmates, with whom he soon grew unpopular. In this furious frenzy of work, he sought to beat down his yearning for everything else; and in it, he succeeded. By night, he was so exhausted from work, he felt little need to talk to Schramek. He toiled on blindly, without ambition, only in order to numb himself, to forget all he had to do without.

He discerned that in this fever of work lay a marvelous mystery, one by which many deceived themselves as to their lives' empty futility; and he hoped to be able to impose a meaning on his own life as well – forgetting, to be sure, that initially youth does not really seek the meaning of life but life itself in all its variety.

One evening when he was a little early getting home from his studies, it occurred to him to step across to the door of his friend, whom he hadn't seen for days. He knocked. No one answered. But he was used to that with Schramek, who often slept in the evening after squandering the night before with his friends.

Now, as he opened the door, the dark room seemed empty to him. But then . . . Something stirred in the leather armchair there by the window . . . A large and laughing girl, who'd been sitting in Schramek's lap, sprang up.

Right away, Berger wished to leave. They must have heard his knock. He blushed with embarrassment. But Schramek sprang up too, seized him by the arm, and pulled him in.

"You see? It's him. He's as scared of a girl as he is of a spider. Oh no, there's no running away. So Karla, you see. This is the Bubi, the one I've told you about."

"I don't see him at all," laughed a bright and rather loud voice.

Indeed, it was much too dark. Berger saw only vaguely, shimmering in the dusk, two shining eyes and white teeth.

"So. Let there be light," Schramek said as he lit the lamp.

Berger felt quite uneasy – his heart was pounding restlessly – but now there was no chance of running away.

He had already heard of this Karla – some jolly thing who worked in a store. She'd been Schramek's girl for a couple of weeks. Alone at times, in his room, he had heard them laughing and whispering; but his shyness had made him unsure as to how to arrange to meet her yet.

The light flared up. Now he saw her standing, tall and pretty: a broad and strong and healthy girl with ample figure, fiery red hair, and big, laughing eyes. A ripe young thing, rather like a servant girl and sloppy, too, in her hairstyle and dress – or had Schramek only rumpled it? It almost looked so. But her lively, uninhibited way was nice as she came up to him, reached for his hand, and said hello.

"So. How do you like him?" asked Schramek, preparing himself for some fun at Berger's expense.

"He's prettier than you," Karla laughed. "It's just too bad he can't talk."

Berger blushed and tried to speak. Yet before he could force out a word or two, Karla laughed and leapt toward Schramek.

"You see? He turns red when you talk to him."

"Let him be," said Schramek. "He can't bear the girls. He's just so shy. You'll confuse him."

"Of course I would. But that wouldn't be bad. Come here, then. I won't bite."

She took hold of his arm to force him to sit.

"But Fräulein," stammered the helpless Berger.

"Did you hear? He said 'Fräulein.' *Fräulein.* You, my dear Mr. Bubi. My name's not Fräulein; my name is Karla, once and for all."

Schramek and Karla laughed boisterously. Berger sensed that he must have looked helpless. Not wanting to seem pathetic, he too began to laugh.

"You know what?" Schramek said. "We'll get some wine. Maybe then he won't be so shy. So Bubi, come on. Stand me a bottle, or better, two. Will you?"

"Of course," Berger said.

Bit by bit he was feeling more sure of himself; they'd just overpowered him so, at first. He went out and called the landlady, who fetched some wine and glasses; then all three of them sat round the table, laughing and chatting. Karla, who'd plopped down next to Berger, toasted him. He had grown visibly braver. At times, when she turned to speak to Schramek, he dared to look right at her. He liked her better now. Her fiery red hair, against her sheer white neck, presented a tempting contrast. And then her freely-flowing vitality – her strong, wild, vital energy – took hold of him, and again and again, he could not help eyeing her sensual red mouth, which sprang open whenever she laughed to reveal her strong and snow-white teeth.

Once, turning to him with a question, she caught him staring at her so.

"Do you like me?" she asked in her lively way. "I like *you*!"

She said this with no attempt to harm, with no attempt to flatter, either; and yet it pleased him somehow – almost, for a moment, made him ecstatic.

He grew more and more animated. And by and by, like a boiling spring, all the submerged spirit of his teenage years welled up in him. He began to tell stories, to clown around. Fired up by the wine, all he said now gleamed with a wild youthful zest even he had not known was in him.

Schramek, too, was amazed.

"But Bubi, what's become of you? See? You should always act like this – and not be such a softie!"

"Yeah," Karla laughed. "Haven't I said the same to you? I'll drag it all out of him."

The landlady had to fetch more wine. The threesome's merriment mounted. Berger, who seldom drank, felt transformed by this rare festivity, as if by a miracle. He laughed and joked confusedly and lost every trace of his shyness. With the third bottle, Karla began to sing.

Then she invited Berger to address her with the familiar "Du."

"It's all right, Schram, no? He's such a sweet guy."

"But of course. Go on! The kiss of brotherhood!"

And before there was time for Berger to think, he felt two moist lips on his mouth. It gave him neither pleasure nor pain but somehow transpired without feeling now in this wild and already faintly misty merriment, which tossed him this way and that. He had only one wish, and it was that this should go on – this zany and lovely hoopla, this gentle euphoria effusing forth from the girl and his youth.

And Karla's cheeks, he noticed, were flushed. And he saw her laugh and wink at Schramek more than once.

Suddenly Schramek said to Berger: "Hey. Have you seen my new saber?"

Berger had no interest in that. Yet Schramek pulled him over. And, as they both knelt down, Schramek said to him gently:

"So, Bubi. We don't need you now. Get lost."

Berger stared at him for a moment, confused. Then he understood. And he said good night.

As he stood in his room, he felt a faint shaking under his feet. His blood hammered in his forehead. Fatigue soon hurled him into bed.

The next morning, for the very first time, he slept straight through his lectures.

This encounter, as fleeting as it was, had beamed a faintly flickering excitement into his blood. He pondered vaguely: was it not some mistake – some mysterious lie – this thirst for friendship? Could it possibly be that, from loneliness, this craving for a wild intimacy was stirred by some other ardent – yet veiled – desire?

He thought back to his days with his sister. Indeed, he mused on those mild blue evenings she used to sit in the garden at dusk, when he could no longer see her face but only the faint white shimmer of her clothes in the twilight while, at times, a cloud still tenderly shone in the night-shrouded sky. What had made him so blissfully happy then, when this voice with its precious words had beckoned to him from the dark, silvery and soft, often blinking brightly from laughter and then again full of tenderness? What had it meant when this music had flown to his heart like a soothing, caressing wind or trusting bird? Had this been only sibling intimacy, or was there not concealed therein – somewhere down in the deepest depths and cooled through a friendship free of desire – a reveling in the feminine, a most sweet and affectionate feeling of womanliness? And was not, perhaps, everything that he vaguely longed for here a kind of glimmer – an errant trace – of the feminine spirit over his life?

Ever since that evening he'd known it for certain: he longed very much for a woman – not so much for a love affair, a relationship, as for some light contact with the female sex. Wasn't all this unknown essence, all this miraculous something he hoped for, somehow linked to women? Were they not the guardians of every mystery, alluring and promising, desiring and desirable at once?

He now began to observe the women out on the street. He saw many who were young and lovely, many whose eyes bore that gleaming light that betrayed so much. To whom did they belong, these ones who so buoyantly strode as in a light dance; who gazed all round them, so proudly upright; who idled in carriages like queens, nestled in their voluptuousness and glancing lazily at everyone who stood outside and gaped at them in amazement? Did longing not live in them as well? And must there not be, behind all those doors – behind the countless and anxiously-veiled and yearning windows of the great city – hundreds of women in whom a desire like his also lived, flowing toward him with arms open wide? Was he not young like them? And hadn't the very same longing been poured into all?

He now went to his lectures less and roamed the streets much more. He felt that he'd finally have to run into someone – someone who could read the trembling sign in his eyes. Some chance incident would have to help him; something unexpected would have to occur. He watched with envy and wild desire as, right in front of him, other guys grew familiar with girls. He saw, on his evenings in the park, countless couples in love, tenderly lost and intertwined; and the yearning to have a love of his own grew more and more urgent to him. To be sure, he sought nothing wild – just a female tender and mild like his sister, loving and dear, true with a childlike sincerity, and with her same bright, gentle voice in the evenings. The image filled his dreams.

Going home each day down the Florianigasse, he came upon swarms of younger girls. They were fifteen or sixteen years of age, and they came from school in little chattering troops. They had all the skipping stride of girls in those years, restlessly peering round and giggling and swinging their books. Every day he watched them from afar – the fresh, laughing faces; the slender bodies in their short skirts; the lightly swaying hips – watched the careless, still-childish happiness with a burning longing to learn from these youths their laughter and merry clarity. And they already knew him. When he appeared, they pushed and teased one another in that special way of teenage girls. They laughed much too uproariously, and they eyed him challengingly, with lively eyes that glanced away as they hurried across the street. Then, as they noted his shy dismay, his bashful turning-away from their stares, they grew more and more brazen from day to day while he lacked the nerve to compose himself and speak to them. Were they not more like boys – like men – than he? Was he not, in all his confused and childish shyness, more like a girl?

He recalled a prank that his sister had played back home a few years before. While he'd been taking a nap, she'd secretly dressed him up as a girl; and when he'd awoken, she'd led him, stumbling, out to her girlfriends, who at first had not recognized him. Then they'd gathered round him with glee and all kinds of jokes. Still a boy at the time, he'd stood there, shaking and blushing. He'd hardly dared to open his eyes and look in the mirror they'd shoved him before. He'd been shy and cowardly even then . . . But then he was just a kid. Now he was nearly a man. And still, he did not know how to be strong and brutal as life required. Why couldn't he be like Schramek – and like Schramek's friends? Was he really, truly inferior – despicable like some kid?

That scene came back to him over and over: how he'd stood there dressed like a girl – how he'd stood there and hadn't dared look up – in the midst of those cocky, cackling creatures. What had become of them since then? They knew all the loving and kissing; they wore long dresses; several had husband and child by now. They'd all stormed out of that room, out of childhood and into *life*. He alone stood ever there – alone in that godawful room – a maiden more than a man, a blushing kid in a lonely room with lowered eyes that did not dare look up . . .

Once (it was late in January), he went to Schramek's room again. He went more seldom now – ever since his lonely prowls through the streets had led him on with their gentle allure. The weather was bleak. The snow of the day before had melted, but the wind remained so biting and sharp that the streets were nearly deserted. Clouds rushed over the steel-gray sky, which stared like someone blind. A stinging rain, which pierced the skin like slivers of ice, began to stream down.

Schramek hardly said hello to him. He was always inconsiderate and rough whenever something in his affairs was amiss. He paced up and down without cease, puffing over and over at his pipe.

At times he turned round curtly, as if about to speak.

"Damned thing," he snarled between his teeth.

Berger sat still. He didn't trust himself to ask what had actually happened. He just knew that Schramek would tell him.

At last the other let loose.

"Such lousy weather. That's just what I needed. And now I've got to go out into it – and all because of these stupid things!"

He paced angrily up and down again, drawing a line through the air with sharp puffs of his pipe. Now Berger asked gingerly: "So what's wrong, then?"

"Oh, this oaf of a fraternity brother of mine goes out and insults two guys yesterday. It'll come off at four today, and then tomorrow again. And I've got an exam at eight and other things to look after. Along with all that, he's picked two who'll surely rip him to shreds – the twit, the fool. If I fail the exam now, that's it. I'll have to sit and wait a year, like the boobs in school. But I shouldn't get all riled up about it, now, should I?"

Berger said nothing. It hadn't taken him long to see the idiocy behind all these duels with their false and easy and gilded gleam – especially now that he'd watched one of them in a dingy and filthy bar – especially now that he'd been to a drinking bout and seen the guys all gray and pale and wasted there in the dawn light after their "ceremonies." He could only smile at the earnestness with which these things were conducted, for he now lacked all interest in them. To be sure, he'd never dared to say this to Schramek, for whom it was in the blood. So they both sat silently there, each absorbed in his private thoughts, while outside the wind rattled louder and louder.

Then the bell rang. And right after that came a knock on the door.

Karla entered, her hat lopsided, and wet strands of hair on her laughing face.

"Lovely out there, no? What do you say? Hello?"

She went up to Schramek and kissed him. He shrugged her off irritably.

"Afraid I'll get you wet with my jacket, you numbskull?"

Then she noticed Berger.

"Hello, Bubi!"

She took off her jacket and tossed it onto the sofa. All were silent. Berger was somehow ill at ease. Ever since that evening they'd drunk to their brotherhood, he'd been with Karla a couple of times, but never again with the same free and open naturalness. The warm erotic wave that had rippled over his life since then made him agitated and restless now in a woman's presence. He almost feared his own passion.

And Schramek did not speak. He was in a nasty mood – couldn't shake the duels, the exam from his mind. The silence stretched out painfully.

Karla now looked rather cross.

"Seems that I've come at an inconvenient time for you gracious sirs. Seems that I've taken the afternoon off just to watch how both of you sleep with your eyes open. So be it, dear people. I have to say that."

Schramek stood up and grabbed his winter coat.

"Dear child, you always come at a convenient time; you know that well. Only not right now. I've got to run. It's half past three, and the duel's set for four, way out in Ottakring."

"Serves him right, the scamp, for being so cheeky with everyone! So you want to run off. What's supposed to happen to me in the meantime? Should I roam the streets in this weather till it's over?"

"Dear child, I won't be back till seven. But you can stay here."

"What should I do then? Sleep? Thanks a lot! That was my concern from nine last night till early this morning. Take me with you. I'd like to see how one gets ripped to shreds in these things."

"What are you thinking? You know that can't be done."

"Well, in God's name, then, I'll just stay here and wait for you. Bubi'll stay here with me. Won't you, Bubi?"

Berger did not know how to respond. He was helpless against such an assault. He hardly dared to look at them. And they began to laugh at him.

"Of course," said Schramek, in a good mood again. "Of course I should leave you two alone. Have you any idea what kind of a coward Bubi is?"

"That's not Bubi at all. He's just a little girlie."

Now they laughed again. How they despise me, Berger thought. Why couldn't he laugh right along with them now? Why was he so clumsy about finding a word, a joke – anything at all? A feeling of rage rose up in him.

"So then. He's fine," Schramek said. "I'll risk it. But what will I do if you two get up to something?"

"It takes two for that."

"As well you know . . . you . . . I'd rather not swear by you."

"I didn't mean *me* at all."

And now they laughed again – with that full, merry laugh of healthy lives that meant no malice yet stung Berger like the strokes of a whip. To be away, just away – a thousand, ten thousand miles, he felt dully. Or to be able to be merry like them. Just not to sit like this without saying one word. Just not to be so clumsy and shy, so confused like a kid, without even the pleasure of feeling sorry for himself.

Schramek put on his cap. "All right, we'll try it. But you'll be sorry if . . . I'll be back at seven. Behave yourself, Bubi. I'll see it in your eyes if you've been up to something. And don't bore the poor girl. See you!"

He grabbed Karla crudely by the hips, so that she turned round, giggling. Then he gave her a pair of rough kisses, waved at Berger, and was gone. The outside door slammed shut.

Now they were alone. Karla and Berger. The wind danced with the rain over the streets; at times, it crackled inside the old stove as if snapping something in two. The room grew more and more silent; the thin breathing of the pendulum clock next door could even be heard. Berger sat there as if asleep. Without looking up, he felt as if she were smiling at him. He felt this look like an electric tingle that lightly touched his hair and raced on down to his toes. He felt as if he would suffocate.

She sat there with her legs crossed, and waited. Then she leaned forward, with a faint smile. And at once she spoke to him there in the silence.

"Bubi! Are you scared?"

Yes, that was it. How did she know? He felt fear, all right, and only fear: a dumb and childish fear. But he forced himself to speak.

"Scared? Scared of what? Scared of you, maybe?"

It all sounded coarse – in a way he hadn't meant.

And again the silence trembled throughout the room. Karla stood up and smoothed her dress and fixed her ruffled hair in the mirror. He saw her eyes laugh. Then she turned halfway around.

"Open up, Bubi. You're being awfully prissy. Tell me something."

Berger felt a bitterness growing inside him – toward her but also toward himself – for being so awkward. He wanted to answer her fiercely again, yet before he could, she came up to him, tender and trusting, sat right down beside him and started to beg like a little child.

"Tell me something. Something clever or even dumb. You read in your books all day. You must know *something*."

She leaned forward even more. That was so like her – to be so free and familiar with everyone. But this soft, warm arm on his own arm confused him.

"I can't think of anything."

"It seems to me that nothing really bright and special ever happens to you. What do you usually do then, on such a long day? Just run around, it seems to me. Lately I've seen you here on the streets in the Josefstadt, but you were in a hurry or didn't want to act like you knew me. It seems to me that you were just chasing a girl."

He tried to protest.

"No, no. I don't mean a thing by it. Say, Bubi. Are you really in a relationship?"

She laughed at him without restraint, relishing his dismay.

"Look here, then. He's blushing. I knew right away that you had one, you lily liver. I'd like to have a look at her sometime. What's she look like, then?"

In all his desperation, he knew only one way, time and again, only one way alone to hide his true feelings. He turned coarse.

"That's *my* business. What's it to you? Concern yourself with your own affairs."

"Yet Bubi! Why are you shouting so? I'm really afraid of you."

She feigned to be terribly shocked.

He sprang up. "Don't always call me Bubi, then. I can't stand it."

"But Schramek calls you that."

"That's different."

Karla laughed. His childish rage gave her great satisfaction.

"Just for that I'll say it again. Bubi, Bubi, Bubi – I've said it three more times."

His nostrils quivered. "Cut it out, I said. I can't stand it."

"But Bubi – Bubi!"

He clenched his fists. The blood rose in his face. He was standing one step in front of her. She could hear how he gasped and see how his eyes sparkled threateningly. Instinctively, she stepped back. Then she regained her high spirits. Laughing, with hands on her hips and a gleam in her teeth, she said, as if to herself: "Well, look here! Now the Bubi's getting vicious."

The mocking word struck him like a whip. He threw himself onto her. He wanted to hit her, beat her, somehow punish her, so that she'd no longer mock him. But that tough, strong girl took his fists quite skillfully into his grip and bent them down. His wrists sang with pain in her icy clutch. He couldn't move; she held him as she would have a child or a toy. Their faces were only a step apart – his own, distorted by rage, with tears almost welling up in his eyes; and hers, alarmed but keenly alert and superior, almost smiling. She held him away from herself for a moment, as if he were nothing more than a snapping pup. So tightly did she squeeze his wrists that in the next moment he would have collapsed to his knees. But then she let go and gently shoved him away.

"So now. Be a good boy again."

But he sprang at her once more. It filled him with rage to think that he'd wriggled so weakly within her grip. Now he had to bring her down, to tame her. He couldn't allow her to laugh at him. All at once he seized her now, in the middle of her torso, in order to throw her down. And now they both gasped, breast to breast, she alarmed and amused by his inexplicable rage, he with feverish bitterness and grinding teeth. Over and over, his hands clawed into her girdle-free body, but she also eased back skillfully; over and over, he tore at the ample hips, but she always fended him off. In their wrestling, his face touched her shoulders and breast; dizzied, he breathed in a soft and warm and enthralling fragrance that weakened his arms more and more. He heard, at times, the noisy and shuddering thrusts of her heart and the rollicking laughter that welled up from deep inside her squeezed breast; and he felt that his muscles would all go slack. He shook this strong, boorish body the way one shakes the trunk of a tree; and though, at times, it gently gave way, it never would buckle: it seemed to resist more and more – till the game got much too stupid for her, and she freed herself with two or three moves. Suddenly she pushed him, flung him back, her voice now angry, almost threatening:

"Now leave me alone!"

He staggered back. His face was burning, his eyes were bloodshot, and all was spinning red, fiery red before his gaze. Yet a third time he sprang at her, blindly, without thinking, and flailing his arms like someone drunk.

And all at once it was something different. This wildly radiating fragrance, this rustling of her dress, this heated touch of her supple body – all this had made him berserk. He no longer wished to strike or to punish her but instead to seize hold of this woman who'd roused his senses so. He tore at her, thoroughly burrowed himself into her hot form, embraced her whole body with his feverish hands. He bit thirstily into her dress, in order to press her down. She laughed yet again, gently tickled by his touch, but in her laugh now lurked a stranger, huskier tone. Her whole being seemed more turbulent; her breast heaved with uneasiness; her body pressed against his more vehemently; her strong hands shook more and more restlessly. Her hair had come undone and was fluttering over her shoulder, heavy and sultrily-scented. Her face grew hotter and hotter. In all the scuffling, her blouse had been ripped open a bit; a button or two had popped off; and all at once, with a flash, he had a peek of her ample white breast. He groaned with one last effort, now sensing that she had no wish to resist at all, that instead she wished to be conquered, hurled down, vanquished; but in spite of this, his strength did not suffice. He quivered about on her helplessly; for a moment it even seemed as though she wished to fall back. She lustily rolled her head back, and he saw her eyes gleam with a light he had never known before now. And it was like a caress, a wildly urgent sigh, as she now said:

"But Bubi, Bubi!"

Then he tore at her again, and when she did not back down beneath his skinny and trembling child's hands, he greedily seized her tousled red hair to pull her down with one tug. She shrieked with anger and pain. With a wild and furious push, she hurled his weak body away from her. He flew through the room like some light toy ball.

In staggering back this time, Berger stumbled, then fell with a crash right into the saber, still propped in the corner. A sharp tear ran through his hand and up – high up – his arm.

For a moment or two he lay there, stunned. Then she came over, trembling faintly with agitation, but anxiously concerned.

"What's happened to you?"

When he did not reply, she helped him sit upright, caressing him as she did. There was no malice in her at all. Standing up was difficult, for he'd stuck his hand into his jacket pocket so she wouldn't see how he had wounded himself. He did not want to answer for it. It burned in him like fire, his rage over being so pitifully weak that he couldn't even once defeat one *willing* to be defeated. For a moment he felt he would have to spring at her once more. Yet he also felt, in his pocket, how hot and wet the blood streaming from the wound was . . .

So he stumbled forward, without looking at her, who, shocked, desired to help him. Tears misted his gaze; he hardly saw the door through the moist cloud they made. Inside, he felt all empty, indifferent. All the fire in him was snuffed out. The blood dripped in his pocket; he felt it vaguely; otherwise, everything in him seemed to have shut down. He just groped blindly to the door . . . and out . . . and into his room.

There he fell onto his bed. The lacerated arm hung over the edge. It kept on bleeding; at times, a drop clapped hard on the floor. Berger gave it no thought. Something surged up inside him – as if it would suffocate him. At last he forced it out: a colossal crying fit, a wild and painful spasm of sobs that he buried deep in his pillow. For several minutes, it lashed at his feverish, childish body. Then he felt freer.

He listened. Karla was pacing round in there with deliberately noisy steps. He didn't move. Now the steps ceased. And now she clattered round in the cupboard, drummed on the table – all to draw attention to herself. Evidently she was waiting for him to come back.

He kept on listening. His heart beat louder and louder, but he moved not a limb.

She went on pacing up and down for a while. Then she whistled a waltz and drummed the rhythm along with it again. At last she grew still. After a time, he heard her go out and the door slam shut.

Through the long endless night, and all throughout the next morning, Berger waited for Schramek to come and take him to task over what had transpired between him and Karla. For he had no doubt that Karla had told Schramek everything right away; he just didn't know whether she'd painted it all as a vicious attack or as an absurd and laughable frolic. All night he brooded: how should he respond to Schramek? He worked out elaborate dialogues, highly-detailed debates and exchanges. He devised certain gestures by which he could cut the discussion off cleanly if – by some chance – he could find no way out. And one thing he knew for sure: that their friendship was now touch and go, that everything was all over now or else would have to start afresh, right from the bottom up.

But he waited in vain. Schramek did not come then; he did not come the next day either. Really, that wasn't unusual: Schramek tended to seek him out only when he needed some favor or else was missing something. Otherwise, it was always he who had to visit Schramek to see him. Only to him, the guilt-ridden one, did there seem a reason for staying away, and he waited with a silent and grim defiance that hurt only himself. He was wholly alone in those days. No one came to see him, and now he felt more strongly than ever the degrading sense that no one needed him, no one loved him, no one required his love. And then he doubly felt what this friendship of his still was, in spite of its every disappointment and humiliation.

That went on for a week. Then one afternoon, as he sat at his desk and tried to work, he heard a few quick steps head toward the door. Right away, he recognized Schramek's stride, sprang up; and then the door flew open too, slammed shut again, and Schramek stood before him, breathless, laughing, grabbed both his arms and shook him back and forth.

"Hello, Bubi! If only you'd been there! The rest were all there – only you were absent, because *you* have to drink all day. And that's all right too. Yeah, I've passed, thank God; it was my last exam. In eight days you'll have to call me doctor of law."

Berger was totally baffled. He had thought of everything possible, only not that they would see each other like this again. He could only stammer a few words of congratulation before Schramek broke him off.

"Yeah, yeah, that's fine don't strain yourself. Come on, come over to my place, we've got to celebrate this properly, and I'll have to tell you all about it. So come on. Karla's already there."

Berger gave a start. He felt a sudden anxiety about being together with Karla, who would just make fun of him while he stood there between the two of them, blushing like a schoolboy. He tried to back out.

"You'll have to excuse me, Schramek, but I can't. With the best will, I can't. I've got an awful lot to do."

"You *do*? What do you have to do, you jerk, when I've just passed my last exam? You'll come along and enjoy yourself with me, or else you'll do nothing at all. Come on with you."

He took his arm and pulled him on. Berger felt too weak to resist. He only noted vaguely how much power Schramek still held over him. Schramek swept him along as if he were just a girl; and not till now had he quite understood how a woman could let herself be overpowered, totally against her will, by such a strong and jolly fellow so full of life – and all from the giddy admiration, the dizzying awe of strength. And so would a wife have to think of her husband – as he did now, at this instant, of Schramek: she would have to feel anger, hate, and yet the easy sensation of being mastered by someone stronger, as well. He did not feel himself to be walking at all; he did not at all know how it happened; but suddenly he was in Schramek's room.

And there stood Karla. As he looked at her, she came up, took him in with an oddly warm look that enveloped him like a soft wave; and utterly without a word, offered him her hand. And once more she looked at him – with curiosity – as if at a stranger, someone completely different.

Schramek was fiddling about at the table. He had a need to do something, the urge to talk; the strong fervor of his joyful excitement needed an outlet. When something seized hold of him, he needed people to help him laugh off his exuberance; otherwise he was actually indifferent and rather reserved. But today his whole being glowed with emotion and a wild, boyish joy.

"So what are we having? I can't tell you stories with a dry throat. No wine, eh? Else we won't have fun tonight, and tonight we need to get smashed. Let's brew some tea. An utterly boring, lovely, hot tea. Will you?"

Karla and Berger consented. They sat next to each other at the table, yet Berger did not speak to her. As a locked-up moth will whir through a room, the thought flew hither and thither throughout his head: had it all been a dream — that he'd fought like someone desperate here in this room, with this woman now seated so calmly beside him? He dared not look at her. He just felt how the air around him was getting stifling, how his throat was getting constricted.

Luckily Schramek did not notice. He was clattering round with the cups and saucers, whistling and chattering . . . It pleased him to play the waiter for them; full of high spirits, he served them. Then he plopped down cozily there in his crackling leather armchair and began to give an account of himself.

"So. The fact that I never learned much is something I don't need to tell you two. And how I creep right up to the exam hall there in my pallbearer's suit, and run into Karl, an old friend of mine — you know Karl of course — and when he sees how faint of heart I am, he starts making an effort to cheer me up. But in all my fear I ask him — you've no idea how shabby a decent fellow gets to looking an hour before the exam — I ask him whether it's hard, and what kinds of questions they've asked for the past two years. And when he gives me the first question, I don't have a clue about it and start to get pretty faint. But I quickly beg him to explain it all to me — some bit of constitutional history, it was — and he crams it inside me and comes along to watch me get slaughtered."

What was he rattling on about? Berger couldn't hear; it all came from far off and sounded like words but made no sense. Deep inside, it just kept quivering, the thought that the woman who'd wrestled him, who'd beat him down, was sitting right next to him, and that the woman didn't scorn him, but on the other hand looked at him with this softly embracing, gleaming gaze . . .

All at once he flinched. A finger had now begun to stroke the scar – the scar that still ran red, like a fiery stripe – along his hand, which had lain heedless there on the table. And as he glanced up, startled, he met a question in Karla's look: an almost tender and sympathetic plea. Fire flared right up into his temples; he had to keep a firm grip on his chair.

Schramek kept talking.

"And what do you know, I've hardly sat down, and there it is, the first question, the very one Karl coached me on. I hear some coughing and giggling behind me, but it was suddenly so easy for me that I wasn't angry at all with them, I start blathering on, it runs like melted butter. And once you're already on board, the train goes a lot farther. Lord knows, I talked till my tongue hurt, but I talked."

Berger did not hear a word. He just knew that the finger was stroking the scar again, and it seemed to him that she could have ripped it open with this discreet movement. A fluttering ran over his body. He suddenly tore his hand from the table as if it were a white-hot plate. An angry confusion rose up inside him. But when he glanced at her, he saw that her closed lips merely stirred as if she were asleep while she gently murmured: "Poor Bubi."

It lay round her lips, a soundless word. But had she really said it? Over there sat Schramek, her lover and his friend, wildly talking on, and meanwhile . . . He trembled faintly; a giddiness seized him; he felt himself grow pale. Then, under the table, Karla took his hand quite gently and softly in her own, and placed it on her knee.

Now he felt it again: all his blood rushed up to his face; then it dammed up in his heart; then it all flowed down and scorched his hand. And he felt a soft round knee. He wanted to tear his hand away, but the sinews did not belong to him. The hand just lay there like some sleeping child, some child softly bedded down for the night and swept away in a marvelous dream.

And over there – oh, how far away was this voice in the smoke – this voice of one who was his friend – his friend, but whom he was now betraying – this voice droning on and on in careless glee all about his good luck!

"Most of all, I'm glad the fixer – that cheeky devil – has lost his cash. Just think. He bets everybody I'll fail, and then, when I come out, he's not at all sure what he ought to do. He must have been happy and put-out both, I tell you, his face, the look on his face . . . But what's up with the two of you, then? Have you gone to sleep on me?"

Karla would not let go of his hand. And Berger could only keep thinking: "That hand . . . *my* hand . . . That knee . . . *her* knee . . ."

But laughing, Karla protested.

"No, one shouldn't be speechless when one gets to be such a foul beast as a lawyer. I'd really like to see it then, what it looks like for the one who just sails on through, the one who's got water on the brain."

They both laughed. Berger shook more and more; a secret horror came over him to see how this girl concealed her deceit. She still held his hand with her own closed round it and pressed it so hard that the ring on his finger drew blood. And gently, she drew her whole full leg against his. And as she did, she spoke calmly – so calmly, he shuddered.

"And now tell me: how should such a wonder of God celebrate? If you don't throw us a big, big bash, you're just a spiteful skinflint, sir: freshly-baked. But whatever you do will be nix – no, nothing at all compared to when *Bubi* becomes a doctor. For then: watch out! Things'll really get going!"

And she lay her hip right on his own, and he felt her soft heat. Everything before him began to sway, he was so agitated. And blood shot painfully to his temples.

Then the pendulum clock struck. A thin voice faintly called its "Cuckoo, cuckoo . . ." seven times. That brought Berger to his senses. He sprang up and stammered a word or two. Then someone extended a hand – Schramek or Karla, he no longer knew – and a voice – probably hers – said "Goodbye." Then he gladly breathed a sigh of relief as the door shut behind him.

And then, in the very next moment, as he stood in his room, it all grew clear to him: he had lost his friend. If he did not want to steal from him, he could not visit Schramek anymore, for he felt he would not be able to resist the temptation of this strange girl. The scent of her hair, the wildly passionate spasm in her limbs, the lusty strength – all of that burned in him; and he knew he would not be able to resist if she were to eye him again as she did today, with that faintly enticing smile. How had it all come about – the way he had suddenly grown so lustful, and the fact that, for his sake, she'd deceive Schramek like that – Schramek, that hard, handsome, healthy fellow – whom he secretly envied so? He did not understand it. And he felt neither pride nor delight to know it – just a wild sorrow to know that now he'd have to avoid his friend so as not to cheat him. To be sure, his friendship with Schramek had not become what he'd hoped; he'd grown wise to many things he'd been blind to at first; but now that it was all over, it all seemed much too final for him. For it was the very last thing in Vienna he still possessed. Everything else had slipped away: first his hopes, then his joy in his studies, and now, at last, his friendship. He felt that this hour had made him utterly poor.

Then he heard a noise next door. A giggle – faint at first – then louder. He listened, both hands on his pounding chest. Were they laughing about *him*? Had Karla told Schramek everything? Had all that at the end been just a game set up to tempt him? He listened. No, it was another kind of laugh: one between smacking kisses and heated giggles. And then words – words of love – of which they were not ashamed. Instinctively, he clenched his fists, threw himself onto his bed, and stuffed his pillow into his ears so as not to hear any more of it. A dread seized hold of him – a wild and raging disgust: disgust he'd have liked to spew out. Disgust at his friend, at the girl, at *himself*, for he'd nearly played right along with this nasty game. He felt a strange, blind, weary, and helpless disgust at all of life.

In the bleak days that followed, he wrote his sister:

Dearest Edith,
 I have yet to thank you for your birthday letter. It is tough for me these days. When it arrived, and I read it, and it told me that I was eighteen years old, I felt it had nothing to do with me, as if it were not even true. For I'd have taken as mockery all the words that had to do with the happiness of my freedom and youth – if it hadn't been for your dear hand and script, familiar since our childhood days, that brought them to me. For my whole life's so different here, so utterly different from anything you could imagine, and so vastly different from all I'd hoped for. It hurts me to write all of this to you, but I have no one here to talk to now. For days, I've spoken to no one. At times I follow people on the street and listen in on their talk – just to know how words sound. I'm familiar with nothing, know nothing, do nothing. I'm fighting against the pointlessness of it all. For days now I haven't had any meaningful kind of experience – haven't seen a familiar face – and you don't really know how it is to be lonely right in the midst of a thousand people.
 It's all over between me and Schramek too. Something's happened there, I can't really say, for you wouldn't understand. I hardly understand it myself, for neither of us is to blame; it's just something between us, like a double-edged sword. And now, for the very first time, I know that I've lost him, and he was the dearest friend that I've had here yet.
 And yet one thing I can tell only you – but you're not to tell anyone else. I've quit studying. I haven't been to a lecture in weeks; my books all lie there gathering dust. I don't know why, but I can't seem to study anymore; I've gotten all dull and apathetic; no kind of work attracts me here; for work's not helping me out from under this stifling feeling of loneliness. I don't want to be here anymore. Everything disgusts me. I hate every stone I step on; I hate my room, the people I meet; I breathe this damp, chill, dirty air in agony. It's all smothering me here; I'm going to die. I'm sinking in the mire of it all. Maybe I'm still too young, and I'm certainly much too weak. I don't have any drive, any will; I stand in the midst of all these people here like a kid.

And I know one thing: I've got to get back home. I can't live alone just yet – maybe in a few years. But now I need you and Mother and Father; I need people who love me and are there to help me. That's childish, I know; it's the fear of a little kid in some dark room; but I can't think otherwise. You've got to tell Mother and Father: I want to give up my studies and come on home, become a farmer or clerk – whatever – no? You'll tell them; explain to them; please, do it soon; I feel like the ground here's burning under my feet. I've never known such an urgent need to get back home; but now, in writing about it, I see it all so clear; and I know that I can't do otherwise. I've got to get back to you.

It's an escape, I know: an escape from life, and not my first. Do you remember the day I was sent to high school and walked into class the very first time? The day sixty guys – all strangers – were leering at me with curious looks, eyeing me with arrogant laughs? It was all so bad that I ran back home and cried the whole day and didn't want to go back. I'm still the kid of that time; I feel the same dumb fears, the same burning sickness – for home and for you and for everyone else I love.

I've got to leave, I must. Now that I've forced it out of myself, I feel there's no turning back. I know that a lot of people will smile and laugh at me when I come home – laugh at a failure, rejected by life; I know it'll bring all of Mother's and Father's fond hopes for me crashing down; I know that this weakness is childish and cowardly; but I can't do anything about it. I just feel I can't live here anymore. No one will ever know what I've suffered here in the last several days; no one can despise me more than I do myself. I feel like somebody branded, or crippled, or sick because I'm totally different from all the rest, and – I'm feeling it, writing it all through tears – I'm bad, unwanted, despicable, and . . .

Here he stopped, for he found himself shocked by his wild outburst of pain. Not until now, with his pen pouring out all his feverish emotion, had he noticed just how much he had built up in him – pain that now sought to break out in broad, rushing torrents.

Should he write all of that to her? Should he dump all this onto a mild maiden's heart, disturbing the one good thing he still possessed with a burden no one could take from him? As if from a distance, amid clouds of mist, he saw her face; saw her clear, loving eyes gladly gleam with a smile; saw her lips press together in fright – saw a shudder run over her face and forced tears trickle down her shocked, pale cheeks. Indeed, why disturb this tender life? Why bother it with a crazed cry for help? If anyone had to suffer, it ought to be him – him alone.

He opened the window, tore up the letter, and strewed the scraps out into the dark. No, better to perish quietly here than plead for help. For had he not learned that life crushed all that was frail and unfit? It would work its justice on him as well; it would not spare him . . .

The white strips of paper fluttered down hesitantly into the courtyard and sank like bright stones in fathomless water. The sky was dark and starless. At times, clouds ran brightly over the dark heights, and the wind hurled a damp, rushing air against the sleeping houses. A mild unrest lay in all of it; this steady cry of the wind resembled agitated breathing; and from the groaning windows and shaking trees there drifted a whisper, as if someone there in the dark were faintly muttering his way through a nightmare. And the wind grew stronger and stronger; the clouds flew faster and faster, like sheet lightning over the sky's black cloak. And all at once as he listened he sensed, in all these strange and agitated movements, the fever of those first miraculous nights that usher in the spring.

And then spring came – quite slowly, like a hesitant guest. Berger hardly recognized it here in this strange old city. It had been quite different for him when, for the very first time, the warm spring wind flowed over the pale white fields, when the black clods sprang from the snow and the air grew moist from their scent. Where was that first wild angst when he'd stood and torn the window screen open to feel the wind on his naked breast and hear the groans of the trees that longed for their leaves? Where was his joy in the thousands of little things: the cry of birds in the distance; the flurry of fluffy white clouds; the ground's finely-flowing crackling and clicking; the sticky little boils on the tips of the asters; and the timid leaves when they broke off; then the solitary, the still hueless bloom? Where was the restlessness that used to flicker deep in the blood? Where was the unrestrained and sensual bliss of throwing off one's overcoat and plodding with heavy shoes on the damp, welling earth? Where was the pleasure of storming up a hill and – for no reason – crying out like a bird rejoicing high, high up in the gleaming air?

How silent the spring was here! How robbed of all its force! Or was it in him, this light, sleepy tiredness, this lack of all joy that would not let him feel glad – not let him feel the soft gold sun that warmed the roofs, or the brightening and enlivening of the street? Why did all this touch him so little that he never went out into the Prater or up to the Kahlenberg, which he saw only from afar (though it seemed borne nearer by the supple air)? His movements were all so limited: he never left his neighborhood. He grew more and more fatigued. He sat in the little park of Schönbrunn (usually the haunt of old people and children); he went there to study or read; but his book would not inspire him; so he merely watched as the children played; and he yearned to play along with them, to revert to this bright, carefree stage of his life.

He'd long since given up his studies. Now he just seemed to vegetate, eyeing things with little interest. True, once he tried to rouse himself. He even went down to the hospital. But when he reached the courtyard there with its budding trees that swayed, unperturbed, in the silence (as if they knew nothing of the dreadful and silent fates all around), he happened to forget himself and sit down on one of the benches. And as the sick in their long blue linen gowns stepped out, with that timid way of the freshly-convalescent; and as they rested with calm, weak hands, without smiling or talking, just giving themselves up wholly to the vague and idle sensations of waking life, so he sat there among them, let the sun run over his fingers, and daydreamed. He'd forgotten what he had wanted here; he just felt that here were people, and there, beyond the round archway, lurked a loud and noisy street where others went while here the hours slowly passed and the shadows stretched themselves imperceptibly. When the sick were signaled to go back inside, he gave a start. Had he not been sitting like one of them? Was he not even sicker – and closer to death – than they? Strangely, he craved nothing more than to sit like that and watch the time melt away.

To be sure, in the evenings at times, a kind of wickedness flared up in him. Bit by bit, he let himself go to the dogs: he hung round with loose women, whom he despised because he had to pay for them; he sat many a night in the coffeehouse and brooded. But all of that happened without any thrills or desire, only out of a gloomy angst in the face of his hopeless loneliness. Ever since he'd stopped speaking with others, an angry crease had formed round his lips; and he dodged his own face in the mirror. A few times he tried to pull himself up, but as if overwhelmed by the weight of that utter loneliness looming up in him, he ever fell right back into his dreamy and aimless lethargy.

Yet life called him back to himself.

Once, when coming home late at night – tired, morose, and with that inner angst in the face of the silently waiting room – he noticed that he must have lost his door key along the way. He rang, despite the danger that Schramek and not the landlady would let him in. But then came hurried, shuffling steps. The old woman opened the door and raised her oil lamp to get a look at who was coming in. Then, as the light fell on her tousled locks and her face, which now seemed almost strange to him, Berger saw that her eyes were bleary and red, that her mouth was creased with a look of grief. And shocked, he wondered what had happened. Why was she up at two in the morning?

He questioned her with concern.

"You don't know it, Doctor, but my daughter Mizzi's got scarlet fever. And it's going badly for her, it is."

She gently began to weep.

Berger was startled. He hadn't known any of this. He'd hardly known that this woman even *had* a daughter. Yes, a few times, in the dark entry hall, when he came and went, some slight little thing – some twelve- or thirteen-year-old – had glided past and carelessly blown him a kiss. But he'd never spoken to her or looked at her. All at once it fell heavy on his heart that for months, a mere breath away and parted only by a wall, people had lived who never saw one another, who met their destinies right next to his own without his ever suspecting. He now saw it: he'd sought the trust and warmth of others, yet he himself had slept like a beast. And right next door, a mere child had wrestled with death.

He tried to comfort the sobbing woman. "It'll turn out all right . . . Just try to calm yourself . . ."

And then, more hesitantly:

"Could I possibly see your daughter . . . It's true I don't know that much yet. I'm still just at the beginning, but at least . . ."

All at once a wild longing to study awoke in him; he'd best go open his books . . .

The woman led him on tiptoe to the sick girl, who lay in a narrow room off the courtyard, murky and filled with the smoke from the oil lamps; across from it there was a firewall. Here nothing of spring was known, and the sun only by the weak reflection that streamed at times over from the illumined windows. Now, of course, one could not see at all how humble the room was, for all was blurred in the dim twilight, though in the corner, where the bed stood, glimmered a faint yellow glow. The girl lay in restless sleep. Her cheeks were red with fever; one of her slender arms hung down, as if forgotten, over the edge of the bed; her lips were sunken in; and at first glance, nothing at all in the lovely face betrayed that she was ill, though her breathing was loud and sometimes pained.

The woman gently told him the story, interrupted now and then by her sobs.

"The doctor was here again today to look at her, but he told me nothing at all. This is the third night I've sat up with her; in the day I have to work in the store. Of course the next-door neighbor is here during the day and does help, but it's three nights now that I've sat up with her, and it's getting no better. Lord knows, I don't mind doing it, even if nothing's happening. Still, if she'd just get better."

Again, sobbing broke up her words. A wild desperation marked all she said.

Yet in Berger, a marvelous feeling welled up. For the first time in his life, he felt that he could help someone; for the very first time, he felt a little of his profession's allure.

"Dear lady, it can't go on this way. You're running yourself ragged and not helping your child at all. Now go lie down. I'll stay here with the child tonight."

"But Doctor!"

She raised her hand in a gesture of shock, as if she could not believe it.

"You've got to go to sleep now. You need the rest. Just leave it to me."

"But Doctor . . . no . . . no . . . How could you manage . . . it won't do . . ."

Berger felt a certainty growing in him; from the heaped-up rubble of the previous month, some vestige of self-esteem had welled up inside him.

"It is my job and my duty."

He said this with utter pride, as if in the joy of having found, in some sudden moment in one of the wee hours of the night, the meaning and purpose of his whole lost life.

They did not quibble for long. The woman was more than exhausted; sleep weighed down on her eyes; so she soon gave in. Berger had only still to defend himself against her attempt – in all the wild emotion of her gratitude and devotion – to kiss his hand before he led her into his room, where he put her to bed on his couch. (For the past few nights, ever since the child had come down sick, she had slept on a mattress in the kitchen. All these little – and yet, in her crisis – dreadful things he had not known about now made him see his service not as a good deed but as penance for a grim transgression.)

And now he was sitting beside the girl's bed. What he felt was inexplicable: life somehow seemed to have grown gentler

– as peaceful as this breathing, which now came and went more delicately. He now saw her face clearly for the first time, fringed by a thin circle of light. As long as he'd lived in Vienna, he'd never had the pleasure of feeling the presence of another so intimately – never gazed into another's eyes for so long a time, never learned all that lay in the lines of another's face. As he looked at her so, a memory came to him: something about those lips made him think of his sister, though this face was still childlike, if careworn, and not yet in bloom. A curious yearning crept over him as to how her eyes might look. Were *they* like his sister's? And again, like an accusation, he felt how he'd failed. Why had he ignored this girl – this girl and her mother – like a stranger? Why had he never thought of these two, who lived right next to him? Why had these lips never smiled for him; why were these eyes as strange to him as they were now, shut beneath the shrine of their lids? Why did he know nothing of all that lived in this slender child's breast, which rose and fell in gentle breaths? With care, he grasped the child's weak hand, which dangled over the edge of the bed, and laid it on the bedspread. His touch was as tender as a caress. And then he sat there silently and gazed at her, fretting over the way he'd neglected his studies and vowing to start his life over again, from the ground up. Already dreamy images arose; he saw himself as a doctor, a healer, and his heart warmed with these enticing thoughts. And again and again, his look embraced the pale and childlike face of this girl and held it fast, as if with a look he might guard her fate and protect her threatened life.

All at once the child stirred and opened her eyes – large, sparkling eyes that gleamed feverishly as if shimmering with tears. Her whole face brightened. At first those eyes seemed to wander round in a circle, as if trying to find a spot where they could pierce through the cloud of fever and shadowy dreams. Then they fixed, as if shocked, upon Berger's face. They felt all along his features, as if questioningly, then fastened upon his gaze. The burning lips moved indistinctly.

Berger sprang up and dried her face, heated by fever, and gave her some water. The girl lowered her head, drank hastily, then fell back weakly against the pillows, her eyes fixed on Berger. To him, her stare did not seem quite conscious, yet something of gratitude was mixed in with her astonishment. And now, as he turned and busied himself in the room, faintly trembling before this unfathomable stare, he felt, without seeing, those large, moist, and gleaming eyes follow him everywhere. And when he returned to the bed, they were wide open now, and as he knelt down, the lips stirred – whether to speak or to smile, he could not say. Then the lids shut, and the light in her face went out. And then she lay there again and slept: silent, pale, with softer breaths now.

In this breathless silence, Berger suddenly felt his heart beating quite loudly. An odd sense of joy stirred in him, expanding wildly. For the very first time in his life, he saw himself actively involved with others; it seemed as if someone had called him to something richly rewarding; indeed, it seemed as if, in these last few hours, something great and lovely had come to pass. Almost with affection did he gaze at the girl, this child, the first person who'd ever entrusted herself to him – one whose life he could win, one who could even win his life back for *him*. He gazed again and again at the one sleeping there; and the long, long hours seemed easy to him. He was quite surprised when, all at once, the lamp went out with a sudden, up-springing flicker and he found the darkness gone and the morning already waiting at the window with its first soft gleam.

The doctor came that morning to see the patient. Berger introduced himself as a student of medicine and, not without feeling a painful sense of his ignorance welling up into his throat, asked whether danger was still at hand.

"I don't think so," the doctor said. "The crisis seems over to me. Oddly enough, children are more resistant to these illnesses than adults. It's almost as if, in them, the strength of their still unlived life can work against death to defeat it. So it is with nearly every children's illness: children overcome it, and grown-ups die from it."

He examined his patient. Berger stood by, deeply moved. When he saw how he seized on every word, observed every gesture, he felt profoundly the miraculous power of this profession he'd blandly chosen and ignored for so long. The whole beauty of it all rose up for him like a sudden burst of sun: why, just to step up to a bed and there – like a gift – lay Hope, Promise, maybe even Health! At this moment, his whole life's direction grew clear. He'd be active and useful. Then he'd be a stranger no more. Then he'd no longer be lonely.

And so he completely assumed the role of taking care of the girl. Without making separate arrangements, he restricted himself to observing the illness's phases, to spending his nights, and a goodly part of his days, beside her bed. The crisis had actually occurred that first night. The high fever had eased. He could already talk with the little one, which he did gladly. Stepping out for a while, he brought a few flowers back with him and told her of spring, which was now already in the Schönbrunn Park, where she usually played. There the trees were gently turning green; there the other girls were already wearing their bright spring clothes. He spoke to her of the sun outside. He told her stories; he read to her; he assured her of a speedy recovery. He knew no better pleasure at all than seeing that she was happy. He grew quite free with these knowingly childish and naïve talks. At times he even surprised himself with his loud and merry laugh.

And that pale little girl just lay there against the pillows and smiled. She smiled quite weakly; a soft and pleasant line etched itself round her lips, then fled like a breath of air. But when she looked at him, her gaze rested: her quite deep and shimmering gray eyes, finely radiant down to their deepest depths, hung warm and heavy upon his face, without any sense of surprise or strangeness, like a child clinging to its mother's neck. Now she, as well, had the pleasure of talking; and soon she lost her initial shyness.

She demanded most to hear of his sister. What did she look like? Was she big or small? How did she dress? Was she good in school? And was her hair also blond, like his? Could he find a way for her to come to Vienna sometime? For surely it must be lovelier here than the little town with the difficult name that had given her quite a good laugh. And she – had she ever been sick?

This girl was ever finding new questions: pure and simple, childish ones. But they didn't make Berger tired. He answered gladly, and it did him good to be able to talk, for once, of his sister, the one he loved most in the whole wide world. And when the girl asked him about her, he brought in the photograph from his desk.

Full of curiosity, she took the picture in her slender, still quite transparent and lucid child's hands.

"There," – she stroked it quite gently with her fingernail – "that's definitely your mouth. Only you often make an angry frown with it, then you look totally different. Earlier, whenever I'd see you, I was always afraid of you, you looked so scary."

"And now?"

"Not anymore. But tell me. Does she have eyes like yours?"

"I think so."

"And they're as big as yours, no? She must be very beautiful, your sister. Ah, see, she wears her hair just the way I do, all braided round like mine. At first Mother didn't want to allow it. She said it would make me look too old. But I'm not a child anymore. I've already been confirmed."

She handed the photograph back to him, and he looked at her for quite a long time without saying a word. For the very first time, he could no longer find in the picture the features of his memories. Imperceptibly, the fine and delicate features of both his sister and this child somehow had blended in his mind's eye: he could no longer separate them. The smiles and voices of both were now one for him, just as they had joined in his life – combined to become the sole feminine being he trusted and loved being near. Karla's form had utterly faded from his memory; all this time, he'd not thought of her once; and as for that hour he'd spent with her once, well, he now thought calmly of that – as one might a sudden frenzy, a drinking binge, or a stupid thing done in a fit of rage. Forgotten too, were all the bitter and brooding days he had suffered here.

He felt only one thing: that a great happiness had come to him. It seemed to him as if he had traveled a long time in the dark, at dusk, then abruptly, to his delight, had seen a light gleaming from far off, white as a star – a light from a house where he could rest and be welcomed as at home. What had he – the childish, the weak, the despondent one – always wished for from women? To the experienced, he must have seemed too foolish; to the innocent, too cowardly. He was still a helpless being: a fledgling and a dreamer. He'd appeared too early on the scene, been pressed too soon on those seeking life's ripened fruits. But this child here, this girl in whom womanhood was first beginning to bud and yet still slumbering, this one who was still so gentle, without pride or greed . . . Was a life not working its way toward him – a destiny of which he could be lord – a soul he would have the pleasure of shaping; a heart that, unawares, was already bending itself toward him? A dream sweeter than every other up to this point – yet far more real than the vague imaginings of his empty hours – now beat, like a warm wave, at his breast.

And then, the more he looked at her, the more he knew her; and now, when in the wake of her illness, her face began softly to take on color and her youthful countenance brightened, now a tenderness – silent and utterly lacking desire – rose up in him. A merely sibling affection it was, for it was happiness just to be permitted to touch her slender hands, to see a smile bloom on her lips.

Once she was lying there quite still. Both of them had grown silent. And at once a longing came to him even he did not understand. He stepped up to her bed, believing that she was asleep. But she merely lay still, smiling strangely at him, her eyes filled with such a radiant light . . . Her lips lay as still as the pale, curled petals of a rose. And at once he knew what he wanted: to touch this mouth with his lips – quite, quite softly – and only once.

He knelt down. Yet even before this sick young child, he was still disheartened. He still lacked the courage.

She looked up at him. "What are you thinking of now?"

Then it seized him; no longer could he be silent. Quite softly, he said: "I would like to give you a kiss. May I?"

She lay there unmoving and only smiled – smiled deep into his heart with her radiant eyes – smiled no longer like a child, but a woman . . .

He bent forward and softly kissed the tender, innocent mouth of the child.

A few days later, the girl was given permission to get up for the first time. In an easy chair placed by the window for her, she sat, quite happy to escape the bed. Berger sat beside her and looked at her proudly. In secret he felt that *he* had saved her – that thanks to him, she belonged to life again. She seemed to have grown some during her illness; the look of a child had softly slipped away: she sat there like a young maiden. Her joy was no longer that of some lively kid, but ever so thoughtful and deeply felt. When she tapped at the window to point to the gleaming sky, when she said "Spring really should come to *me*, if I can't go out yet," it seemed to Berger a minor miracle, one of life's never-noted little sweetnesses. And no longer was he ashamed of himself for being in love with a thirteen-year-old girl, for he knew that all this – all this joy he'd known in these days of her convalescence – was, in a sense, quite dreamlike and irretrievable. And it gripped him wondrously, this cheerful, familiar affection she had for him, this hearty confidence not at all marred by feminine modesty. She often called him by his first name now, and he felt, in the midst of high spirits, a blissful sense of no longer being alone. Laughter leapt from his soul again; he considered it as he might a forgotten lingo of childhood days. And when he was alone, gentle reveries came; he saw her as a grown woman:

clever, solemn, sensible. And he saw himself in these images, too – saw himself and knew she would grow and become a woman for him.

But his loneliness ceased in another way too. The girl's mother looked up to him as she would a god. She seemed to spend her whole day devising ways she could show him her gratitude. And now, from time to time, as he spoke with her, he marked that this woman had suffered many misfortunes and yet, in spite of humiliations and disappointments, had preserved a triumphant goodness. He now regretted the way he had curtly dismissed these people as underlings. He was glad he had since paid his debt to them.

And he found his way back to Schramek again, as well. He met him in the hallway once, and Berger was amazed with himself to find how cheerfully and easily he could chat with the other now. They talked of Karla, and the mention of her no longer pained him. There was too much heartfelt joy in him, a freedom of movement and being that flowed right into his stride and made it upright and supple. Life was getting through to him from all sides; everything fit with everything else; and the one desire that wildly urged him on was to crack those dusty books and begin his studies. His calling lured him now with a golden gleam. He just wanted to wait a couple of days – till the girl would be completely well. He felt a need to make the most of this first success, to feel the pleasure of every last second of these wildly glorious days.

For the past two weeks, he'd hardly been out. He'd dashed out of the sick room only at times – to take care of this or that. And now, as he ambled along the gleaming sun-soaked cobblestones, he felt completely, for the very first time, the spring, whose cool and fragrant breath quivered over the splendidly shining city. And, as it rose up glittering from the cloudy wet mist, he seemed to be seeing this city, too, for the very first time. He saw these old houses of the Josefstadt, which had always seemed rundown and grimy to him, in all their homely intimacy now that a brilliant blue sky keenly outlined their ancient chimneys and roofs; he felt, far beyond the broad streets, the distant Kahlenberg greeting him, its greenery still quite pale. Everyone seemed to wear a brighter face. The women he passed now seemed to give him a friendlier look. Or was it only the gleam from deep in him, reflected back from everything, from the glossy dark eyes and the glistening streets, from the flickering windows and, freshly-awakened, the gaudy flowers behind their panes? All around him no longer seemed so alien and hostile but instead lay there like a richly-hued and ripening fruit that promised speedy possession and all the marvelous foretaste of pleasure. Again and again, a fresh abundance flowed from it all, bearing him forth like a wave. He gave himself utterly to his joy.

Soon a gentle numbing came over him. His feet grew heavy, as if he were drunk; his head felt leaden yet seemed to spin. He felt a sudden giddiness – like spring fever. On the Ringstrasse, he had to sit down on a bench. Before him, upon his hands and his gently shivering body, streamed the sun, whose rays – not filtered by thick foliage yet – now swelled and surged with such a force that he had to shut his eyes. Noisy crowds stormed past on the cobblestones; people scurried all round him; but something compelled him to keep his eyes shut and stay slumped on the hard, cold bench, without moving. He sat like that for two to three hours. Not till twilight, when the chill set in, did he rouse himself and head back home, but with difficulty, like someone sick.

He went past the room where the girl was. He felt the need to be alone for a while – now that he'd reconciled himself, at last, to the richness of this new beginning, to the marvelous change of these last few weeks. He sat down at his desk to set his books and papers in order. In the morning he'd get back to studying again.

A thick notebook fell into his hand; he hardly recognized it at first. Its pages were blank. Ever since his arrival in Vienna, he had meant to keep a journal. But he'd always waited for an event that was worthy enough to write about on the very first page. He'd waited, and finally, as the days had grown ever more tedious, he'd forgotten all about it. Now it seemed to him like a sign. For only now had he begun to live. Only now had stars begun to shine in his desolate night. This would be a journal of all his experiences and – he felt this with some uncertainty – perhaps a journal of love. For inside him spoke some voice that said his affection for this child would turn into a love for a woman someday . . .

He turned the lamp up high. Then he took inks of black and red and all sorts of pens and on the first page began to inscribe, with many flourishes and arabesques, Dante's words: "*Incipit vita Nuova.*" Ever since childhood, he'd loved to play around with fancy writing like this; and here too, where his past and future would both be recorded, he embroidered lovely curling letters he filled in with red and black. "A new life has begun." That should shine like blood!

There . . . he stopped writing . . . A splash of ink lay on his hand: a little round red spot. He tried to wipe it away. It stayed. He took some water and rubbed it. The spot would not go away . . . How strange . . . He tried again . . . And again, but in vain.

Then a thought raced through him sharply, like lightning. He felt his blood freeze. What was it? What . . .

Anxiously, but with hesitation, he pushed up his sleeve. Then he felt his wandering fingers grow chill. Here too were perfectly circular red spots – one, two, three. At once he understood his earlier fatigue and stress. He knew enough. The hammering in his temples intensified; something caught in his throat. And under the desk, his feet felt strange, like cold, heavy blocks.

He got up, staggering, and passed the mirror with a frightened look. No, don't look there! And nothing would do – not screaming or crying. Nothing to hope for or wait for; it was irreversible. And of course it all made sense. He'd caught it: scarlet fever.

Scarlet fever . . . and then suddenly he heard – as if someone were with him there in the room and saying the words the doctor had said about it:

"Children get over it easier, but grown-ups die of it."

Scarlet fever . . . dying . . . That made it all come together. Scarlet fever: a child's disease! Was it not a symbol for his whole life, that as an adult he'd caught what only belonged to kids and childhood? And adults had a harder time surviving it than kids: how well he understood that now!

But the thought of death – he rebelled against it all too much. Three weeks ago – how gladly he'd have gone then; how quietly and inconspicuously he'd have slipped off this stage where no one belonged or spoke to him. But now? Why had life played with him so, showing him tempting things in his very last hours in order to make his farewell so hard? Why now, when he'd just got connected with people again, when many others would suffer perhaps – perhaps even more than he would?

Then the weariness came over him: a dumb, stunned resignation. He stared at the round red spots till they danced like sparks before his eyes. All grew confused for him. He still just felt it had all been a dream. Good luck or bad; going or coming; being with people or being without them – none of it mattered. He no longer yearned for anything. Was this dying, he thought with agony – just getting all quiet and apathetic like this?

Yet he still wished to take his farewell.

He went into the room where the girl was sleeping. With one glance, he took in the resting and so familiar features. Had he not dreamed that his destiny would be here? And had it not been for him through her – only quite, quite different from what he had thought it would be – not life at all, but death?

He tenderly stroked the girl's features with his gaze. And that smile that faintly rimmed her childish mouth in sleep – he took that smile upon his own lips. To be certain, now, as he stepped from the room, it already hung down bitterly, like a wilted bloom.

He tore through a couple of letters and wrote an address on a slip of paper. Then he rang and waited.

The old woman came dashing in right away. (She was always blowing in like that – in order to be of service to him, whom she idolized.)

"I –," he began.

But he had to start over, his voice not quite firm.

"I don't feel very well. Please get my bed ready for me and call the doctor. If it should go badly for me, send a telegram to my sister. Here's the address."

Two hours later, he was lying in a heated fever.

The fever burned frightfully in his blood. It was as if the strength of his unlived hours, of his still unexpended passion, would be burned up in him in the mere two days he would still be granted from a life that should have been long.

The whole house was distraught. The girl crept round him with tearful eyes and dared not meet those of anyone else, afraid she might be blamed. The old woman knelt in despair before the crucifix in the entry hall and prayed for the young man's life. Schramek came to see him repeatedly and, with his indestructible confidence, assured them that everything would turn out all right.

The doctor thought otherwise and had the telegram sent to Berger's sister.

For two days, the fever held Berger, unconscious now, in its grip, tossing him up and down in its crimson billows. He woke once more. His blood had grown quite still. He lay motionless there, his hands weak, his eyes shut.

But he was quite awake. He felt that the room must now be very bright, for it lay like a rosy red fog on his eyelids.

He remained motionless. Then the bird next door began to twitter – quite carefully first, as if to test him – then it really got going: rejoicing, trilling a tune that rose and leapt up and down. Berger listened. It vaguely occurred to him that it must be spring.

The voice of the bird rang louder and louder; its elation almost gave him pain. It seemed to have nested here in his bed beside him and was purling this shrill sound into his ear . . .

But no . . . Now it was utterly soft again, so distant. It must be perched in a tree, outside, in the spring. The song grew ever softer, ever more tender, as if from a flute; was that not the fine silvery-supple voice of a girl: the bright, sweet voice of a child?

A girl, a child . . . Memories came timidly drifting back to touch his heart. All of it slowly came back to him, but not in the proper sequence – just images drifting one after another. The smiling child's voice rose up from the darkness of oblivion; and now, shadowy yet sweet, that single stealthy kiss. And the illness then, and the mother, the whole house – the whole round of experience ran all the way back and he suddenly knew that he lay there sick and might die.

He opened his heavy eyelids. He was utterly alone. The bird next door was no longer singing; and the clock, which normally ticked away busily, was also still; someone had forgotten to wind it back up. His eyelids slowly slid shut again, without his noticing.

He looked back at the room as if from a distance and there he was on his first night here, whining as the rain rushed down, feeling all bitter, abandoned. Then all of it came back again: Schramek and all the other crazy things, but now it was all quite unreal . . . So strange . . . It did no good, but it didn't hurt. It just ran past in the great big dullness.

Then at once . . . next door . . . He heard a door shut. And then a few steps. He recognized them: they were Schramek's. Yes. That was his voice. To whom was he speaking? The blood in his temples began to tick . . . Wasn't that Karla now, laughing next door? Oh, how that laugh hurt. She ought to be quiet now! He wanted calm . . . silence . . . stillness. But no, what were they doing? He heard her laugh. And at once, as if through glass, he saw her there in the room. There stood Schramek, who held her and kissed her. And with laughing eyes, she wiggled her hips, as she had back then, just as back then . . .

His hands were feverish. Why were they laughing so madly over there? It pained him so. They didn't know that he might die here, that he *was* dying here, completely alone, without a friend. He felt tears rising; something was seething in his breast. He waved his hands all around him. Couldn't they wait till he was dead? But then . . . a chair crashed to the floor . . . He saw everything, how she sprang from him. And now, as he ran toward her, how wild, how strong he was, how he grabbed her, jumped over her and the table . . . And now she was gone again . . . Where? Yes, she'd hidden, then . . . And now they leapt and ran around. The room began to shake . . . Wasn't the whole house roaring now . . . Yes, everything swung here and there; a terrible noise filled the air. Why wouldn't they calm down now, in his very last hour, damn them! No, they kept on running, and he kept on chasing them – no, now, he'd caught them.

"Why do you scream in your lust and angst like that?" Berger groaned bitterly. He'd now grabbed hold of Schramek, whose loosened red hair ran down like blood . . . Now he tore off her coat . . . Her blouse shone white . . . She herself was utterly naked and white . . .

And so they chased one another round the table – here, there, here, and back . . . How she just laughed – laughed and laughed!

How had *that* happened? In the midst of it all, she'd blown right through the wall and into his room and now was standing before him . . . before his bed . . . gleaming white . . . and naked . . . or . . .

With pain, he opened his heavy eyelids – or . . . Was that not his sister, dressed there in white, standing before him there? Was that not her lovely cool hand on his brow?

The fire burned for two more hours. Then it went out. At his bed stood his sister, the child, and Schramek – the three he had loved and who now were joined in this way to signify his whole life. None spoke a word. The little girl sobbed faintly; and by and by, this last lament died. The room grew utterly silent; all three were solemn and sad; and nothing was heard but the loud, angry voice of the strange, great city, which rumbled on without cease and concerned itself neither with death nor with life.

AFTERWORD

The five narratives in this collection are set in early twentieth-century Vienna, the city of Stefan Zweig's childhood, youth, and early manhood. The first appeared in print when he was only 19, the last when he was 27. Although Zweig, as the son of a wealthy textile manufacturer, definitely belonged to the upper middle class, these stories feature characters from various social backgrounds. Yet all depict isolated and sensitive young people struggling to adjust to a world that is callous and sometimes brutal. As such, they foreshadow concerns of Zweig's later fiction, as well as those of his own life and the lives of untold others throughout the twentieth century and after.

Perhaps the most drastic case of a character failing to adjust appears in the aptly-named "A Loser" ("Ein Verbummelter") of 1901. Though not the earliest of the group chronologically, this piece, with its brevity and intensity, serves as a fitting entry into the collection. Like the other protagonists of these stories, Liebmann is clearly an outcast, and the world he finds himself in is definitely insensitive to his needs. It is a world that forces one to conform to certain expectations, one that allows no deviation from established norms, and Liebmann's inability to submit propels him, at last, to violence. Certainly the story demonstrates what Theodor Csokor would later call, in reference to Zweig's 1911 volume *Erstes Erlebnis* (*First Experience*), the "gloomy dangerousness of boyhood" (Beck, *Praterfrühling* 369), for it dramatizes quite memorably the darkness that can brood just under the surface in youth. Though the system that Zweig presents us here, with its peremptory insistence on obedience to authority (as represented by the unyielding schoolmaster), is one that might seem antiquated, the plight of the slow-witted Liebmann, who cannot meet its demands, remains relevant; the drama of a young man straining, and failing, to rein in his bestial impulses is just as timely. One is reminded of similar rebellions in Herman Melville's *Billy Budd* and D. H. Lawrence's "The

Prussian Officer," and yet the master here, though modeled after one of Zweig's own former teachers (Beck, *Amokläufer* 201), seems merely a type who is playing his part in an unfeeling, dictatorial hierarchy. This does not make his (and his more "normal" students') treatment of Liebmann any less insidious. Yet Zweig focuses more on Liebmann's reactions, and what complicates matters is Liebmann's own exaggerated sense of self – no doubt a defense mechanism, but one that is apt to make us smile and thus side, at moments, with his master and fellow students. Skillfully, then, Zweig creates tension, placing us somewhere between the hapless Liebmann and the "system." But the mood darkens when Liebmann, after striking his master, sees his life ruined and himself not as victim, but villain, within that system. Joining those among Dante's damned who wreak violence on themselves, he leaps to his death from a bridge. Although earlier, we might have viewed him as comic, he is transfigured here when Zweig describes him as being momentarily too shaken to summon the strength to hurl himself over the rail, and so, as W. B. Yeats says in another context, "a terrible beauty is born."

The misshapen Jula and her lame companion in "Two Lonely Souls" ("Zwei Einsame," also of 1901) are, like Liebmann, misfits, in their case because of physical, not mental deficiencies. They also suffer the ridicule of their co-workers much as Liebmann does the disdain of his teacher and schoolmates. Yet Zweig's portraits of them are also complex. Knut Beck has noted the connection between this early piece and Zweig's later novel *Beware of Pity (Ungeduld des Herzens,* 1939) (*Praterfrühling* 372); and Jula indeed foreshadows the crippled Edith Kekesfalva of that later work in the way she responds to her condition with understandable self-pity and rage. Yet Jula and her admirer, unlike Edith and Lieutenant Hofmiller in the later work, share a bond because of their handicaps. The old saying "misery loves company" rings true in their case; they are united through joint suffering; and the end is tender yet gently humorous: "All at once she noted, with a vague joy, how his hand reached round her swollen hips in a soft and groping caress." Author and reader alike are implicated by their natural reactions to this odd coupling; we may even chuckle here as we do at Liebmann's pompous self-estimations. But we are also comforted somewhat to know that these two have found at least partial relief from their isolation.

"The Love of Erika Ewald" ("Die Liebe der Erika Ewald," 1904) presents a heroine alienated not because of some mental or physical defect but instead by a sensibility that resists all that is "loud and brutal and ugly in life." Erika finds her work with clumsy music students "torture" and home life with a distant father and spinster sister unbearably stifling. She longs for romance and love, yet unlike the earlier Emma Bovary, to whom she links herself, in Erika we find an industrious young woman respected in music circles, as well as one who shies away from physical passion. This bashfulness in regard to sex might strike us as hopelessly dated, yet in his memoir *The World of Yesterday* (*Die Welt von Gestern*, 1944), Zweig shows it as typical of the young women of his youth (Zweig 78-79). Certainly, Erika is diffident – so much so that readers today might find themselves cheering her tempter on. Indeed, the scenes in the Prater are charged with a tension produced by our natural longing for consummation between the two lovers on the one hand and, on the other, our moral resistance to a union that will surely break Erika's heart. Yet if we smirk to find her briefly praising herself for having escaped "in the nick of time," our baser selves are later gratified when she stoops to our level and begins to long with lust for her would-be seducer. Her newfound desire perhaps makes her more "human" to us, and we are distressed when she confronts him and finds that it is too late: he has settled for a lesser woman. We might be tempted to smile toward the end when Erika warns her students of "fate and its malice," but we find ourselves instantly sobered when we realize that, unwittingly, character and circumstances have conspired to create her loveless fate.

Our final view of Erika (like that of Liebmann) is transformed by the depth of her suffering. And this Zweig explores with an intricacy almost Proustian, so that, by the end of this richly complex novella, we have suffered right along with her and are moved to sympathize with one who likely possesses a far more delicate sensibility than our own. We are also led to accept the grim fact that a life without love is indeed her destiny; one profound loss in love has branded her for good. And yet, we respect her for being not bitter but wistful as she recalls the notes of the air her lost love once played for her.

A loveless fate is also dealt to Lizzie of "Prater Spring" ("Praterfrühling," 1900), which, as Knut Beck has surmised, was quite likely Zweig's first published story (*Praterfrühling* 971). A more different type of woman than Erika could not be found, we might think at first. Yet we also come to admire (and view with awe the destiny of) this woman who stands at the other extreme of the Vienna of Zweig's early manhood. As representative of an industry that Zweig explores in much depth in *The World of Yesterday*, Lizzie leads a life devoted solely to satisfying male libidos. Her work rewards her with earthly comforts: bonbons, a posh boudoir, a "noble" address. Yet while Erika Ewald comes to know the agonies of a love that is purely spiritual, Lizzie is brought face to face with the emptiness of a life wholly carnal. A spring day in the Prater spent with a callow young student allows her the fantasy of living a life once again informed by love. But morning comes, and this Cinderella of sorts must return to her dreary reality of entertaining, monotonously, one admirer after another, the prospect of which clearly "fills her with fright." Still, her memories of the precious day are able, at least temporarily, to blot out that reality. And her awareness that love is still something that she can feel seems to give her the hope to go on. Despite her drastic difference in background and situation, Lizzie, like Erika, is a fragile soul sustained by selective memories, yet one whom we can both pity and respect.

By contrast, in "Scarlet Fever" ("Scharlach," 1908), the last and chronologically latest of the works in this volume, Berthold Berger's nostalgia for life back home is part of what keeps him from facing the realities of city life. As Knut Beck has observed, Berger's experience as a yokel freshly arrived from the provinces mirrors that of the twenty-year-old bourgeois Viennese Zweig in wild, bohemian Berlin (*Praterfrühling* 369). Indeed, as Beck has conjectured, something must have led Zweig to consider "Scarlet Fever" as too personal, for he never included it in collected editions of his fiction (369). Yet whatever reservations the modest young author himself might have held about "Scarlet Fever," and whatever embarrassing resemblances might exist between him and his main character, the fact remains that this novella provides a compelling study of a boy striving, and failing, to reach manhood. To be certain, just as we are inclined to smirk at the self-delusions of the earlier Liebmann, so are we apt to smile over Berger's early misconceptions as to what manhood requires. Yet his desperation makes those smiles nervous ones. His is the plight of someone scrambling in terror to secure a firm footing while poised over the abyss of a pathologically terminal childhood, a desperately-unwanted "girlishness." Still, in this thwarted *Bildungsroman*, we also laud his attempts to mature: the way he eventually sees through Schramek's shallow notions of manhood, the way he yearns for a feminine counterpart in his life who might relieve him of his own more traditionally "feminine" role in relation to Schramek. At first, the buxom Karla seems a ready agent for his initiation into masculinity. Yet he resists sex as Erika Ewald does – not, like her, to preserve his virginity, but to avoid betraying Schramek, whom he pathetically sees as a friend. He, like Erika, acts from a sense of honor that some might now see as obsolete. Yet we agonize right along with both. Their innocence shows us a virtue that all too many of us have lost, and we are moved by our recognition that, in doing the right thing, both tragically suffer self-blame and unbearable loneliness.

    To be sure, toward the end, Berger seems to find a chance at love and manly identity too. Helping the young daughter of his landlady through the last throes of scarlet fever renews his hope in life and himself. Because Zweig's tone grows more lyrical here, we are led to suspect a tender conclusion. Will the innocent love of a budding doctor and his nymph-like Pygmalion flourish? Or will Zweig lavish on us an operatic finale reminiscent of Puccini's *La Bohème*, with the ill young heroine tragically dying? Instead, he surprises us, and at first we rebel against what seems a cheap trick on this young author's part to subvert an emotionally pleasing ending by killing the hero off. On reflection, though, we accept that Berger's naïveté – his feeling that he can guide this girl into womanhood, all the while preserving her innocence – is one last delusion. We may even blame him for being selfish – for wanting to mold her to suit his own needs – and arguably, a cruel poetic justice is served with his death.

Yet Zweig surprises us once again. In a final twist, he indicts not Berger but his world for his fate. We are left, in the end, with "the loud, angry voice of the strange, great city, which rumbled on without cease and concerned itself neither with death nor with life." This world is clearly a Darwinian one, one ruled by the likes of Schramek and Karla. These, as Berger knows, are the "healthy" ones, and readers may recognize counterparts in Klöterjahn and son in Mann's "Tristan" of five years before, or even Gregor Samsa's family members in Kafka's "The Metamorphosis" of five years later. Perhaps one difference lies in that, once again, Zweig plays with our sympathies, and so we fellow survivors are also indicted, for we cannot help *liking* Schramek and Karla despite all their limitations – despite all the ways they have let Berger down – and simply by being the creatures they are. We might even find parallels between Berger's fate and that of Zweig and his frail young second wife (afflicted not with scarlet fever but asthma), who, decades later, hounded and haunted by fascism's specters, took their own lives to escape a world that seemed destined, in the darkest hours of the Second World War, to be ruled by the self-proclaimed "healthy" ones. Whatever the case, Berger's destiny is that of all those too tender and sensitive to adapt to a world that, many would argue, grows increasingly more unfeeling. True, the forces of tyranny have largely been vanquished. Yet even in our largely free world, with all its rich opportunities – all its prospects for friendship and fame and success – the chances for loneliness and defeat can be just as great. Berger's city, in some ways, remains our own.

– William Ruleman

WORKS CITED

Beck, Knut. Afterword. *Der Amokläufer:Erzählungen*. By Stefan Zweig. Frankfurt am Main: S. Fischer, 1985. Print.

Beck, Knut. Afterword. *Praterfrühling:Erzählungen*. By Stefan Zweig. Frankfurt am Main: S. Fischer, 1990. Print.

Zweig, Stefan. *The World of Yesterday*. New York: Viking, 1943. Rpt. in Lincoln and London: U of Nebraska Press, 1964. Print.

Edwards Brothers Inc.
Ann Arbor MI. USA
February 24, 2011